What's in a name is a conundrum that has nagged at people for years. But never has it been more real than in Shirley Wilson's new short story collection, *Something about a Name*. In these twenty-five entertaining and engaging stories, there are important memories, love stories, adventures. People who can't live up to their names. People who deplore their names. People who discard their names. There are people who are deeply sorry about the choice of a name they gave their children.

Some stories deal with name changes and what it can mean to a character's life. Some with the pronunciation of a name. Some with a name made famous.

It is difficult to have a favorite when all of the stories are so beautifully written. But I think when Myrtice buys a cemetery plot and happily envisions her own name on the future headstone, that is the zenith.

—Doris Gwaltney
Author of *Homefront*
and *Treason's Daughter*

Something about a Name

Short Stories
by
Shirley Wilson

Something about a Name

A Short Story Collection
by
Shirley Wilson

Live Wire Press

Edited by Patricia Adler
Live Wire Press
www.livewirepress.wordpress.com

This book can be ordered from your local bookseller
and online at Amazon.com

ISBN 978-0-9861713-3-8

10 9 8 7 6 5 4 3 2 1

Printed in the United States

To my daughters

Table of Contents

Solomon

Solomon curled his hand into a fist in his lap, squeezing it over and over again. Then he reached up and turned off the big machine with a harsh flick.

"Don't be calling me out of my name," he said, his voice deep and sonorous.

The foreman turned to the others and yelled, "You guys get back to it," but the three men who had stopped their work on the bridge to see what Solomon would do, didn't budge.

"I said, get back to work!" the foreman yelled again.

The men could see Solomon easing off the Cat machine, just behind the foreman, and they couldn't move. When he started forward, one of the men said in an even voice, as if talking to a child, "Sol . . . you don't want to. . . ."

But Solomon raised his hand and pushed the air hard with the pink palm of it. He looked like a chieftain, halting a multitude of people.

Somebody else said, "Hey big man, it ain't worth it."

Then the look on Solomon's face rendered them all silent. Even the foreman got quiet. It was Solomon's eyes that were scaring him; something strange and powerful was welling up in them. *If I could just get to my cell phone*, he thought, *I could call for help.*

"You called me out of my *name*," Solomon said, standing close now, a good foot above his boss.

"Now, look . . ." the foreman started. "Whatever that means, I think we can all get back to work, here."

Better watch it, big guy, he was thinking. *You could be replaced by the end of this day.*

The traffic was whizzing by and they all knew how dangerous it was to lose their awareness of passing cars. There had been too many accidents involving construction on this bridge not to be aware. And although the lane they worked on had been partially closed, they still had to watch carefully. The foreman was particularly conscious of the traffic—he had seen out of the corner of his eye that it had picked up, knew it was near peak time for the working population. If something happened now, some accident, it would be on his head. He knew he had to maintain calm. A lone seagull flew directly over them, squawking loud. Other seagulls sat like sentinels on the surrounding light posts, looking down at the men in orange jackets.

One car, booming loud rap, passed, followed by a long, mysterious limo with dark windows. Then an open convertible with four people sped by, their laughter trailing behind like streamers. All the cars had their own particular rhythms, and when they crossed over the median section of the bridge—just beyond the workers—their sounds changed, became a kind of long hum.

Solomon had liked that part of the bridge since his first day on the job some months ago, when he had seen it open and hold up cars for almost a full fifteen minutes on either side, to let a lone boat with tall sails pass. To him it was a good lesson—no matter how busy people got, how important they thought they were, how fast they drove to get to their destinations, a bridge could render them powerless.

He had been glad when he got this job, prided himself on doing it well. He came home that first night and sang out joyously in choir practice, his deep alto punctuating the other voices, lifting them up, bringing them out. And that night he had lain next to his wife, Sallie, with such peace in his heart. All that was calling to him now—the sound of tires on the bridge median was bringing it back—especially thoughts of Sallie and the kids. *But the man had called him out of his name.*

The foreman, known for his quick temper, was also being called by the bridge. But it was the growing traffic that called to him, reminding that big consequences lay in wait, if he did not handle this wisely. He'd have to go easy. The whole thing seemed to him a continuation of the morning's argument with his wife.

"Be careful with your words," she had told him at the breakfast table where her food had not been touched. "Be *careful* what you say to me!"

"Joe," he said, addressing one of the workers he trusted to explain things regarding the others, "Just tell me," he said to the man, but loud enough for all to hear the question, ". . . what this 'calling out of a name' means."

Joe reached up and scratched the back of his neck, and looked away a moment. The other men just glanced at each other. One blew out air through his teeth, as if disgusted with the question.

"Well, it's . . ." Joe began. "It's something you just don't do . . . to *us*." He had overheard the situation and knew what the foreman had called Solomon but wanted to talk around it, not name the word. Most of the others had not actually heard what the foreman said, though they had been aware of an argument.

"A man's got a name, just call him that," Joe said. He knows if he says the word outright it would incite the others—and more, would incite Solomon again. Jobs could hang in the balance. He scratched the back of his neck again and this time gave the foreman a hard, serious look.

"Don't call us *anything* but our name," he said.

The seagulls were quiet, even the traffic seemed to recede to a rumble as they waited. Finally, the foreman slowly nodded his head up and down, acknowledging Joe's answer. Then he turned back to Solomon. The words wrenched out of him, but they were what Solomon had waited to hear.

"I'm sorry," the foreman said. Then added, "Solomon."

Solomon just stared at him for a long moment, then turned and climbed back on the Cat machine.

"Let's all get back to work," the foreman yelled to the others, and the men went back to their riveting.

The seagulls rose and flew away. But the work took on a seriousness now as if the men were also working through the situation—trying to put it all somewhere, on a bridge in Virginia, in the year 2003.

Solomon, up on the big machine, high above the other workers, felt the late afternoon breeze from the river on his face and slowly began to hum away the word. The bridge was looking good, the work was good, he thought. He had told Sallie just last night that if he only had the education he would have liked to design bridges. There was something about the way they were put together, he told her, that seemed such a wonder.

The foreman could still feel sweat rolling down his back, under

3

his shirt. Sweat that had come more from fear than the sun. He thought back to how it all started. They had argued about how to finish up the job, and Solomon had tried to tell him—the *boss*—the "best" way to do it. As if he knew! And somewhere in all that, he had called him "Boy." Must have slipped out, he thought; he had not done that in years. But you would think, he told himself, by the way they all acted, it had been the "n" word.

He had the comfort of his cell phone now. He toyed with it for some time, watching Solomon handle the Cat machine with deft hands, thinking of the report he had to make at the end of the day. He decided not to relate the incident.

He put some numbers into the phone and waited, looking out over the river. A tug boat was making its way to the shipyard, cutting a path through the sun's crimson rays.

"Jane," he said when his wife answered. The words—broken in now—came easier this time, "I'm sorry."

Demetrius

People always expected something different from Demetrius. He gave them pause.

His mind went into surprising, imaginative paths that twisted and turned, gathering strength before finally laying bare its deductions. It both delighted and scared his teachers. One of his teachers likened his latest summation to an idea so alive it was "like a caught fish, still breathing, still floundering . . . as if his teeming mind is seeing even more."

His parents, a machinist and homemaker, were totally in awe of the boy, even a little embarrassed at times. His father, when he wasn't too tired, asked him about school or other things, but Demetrius' answers always made him a little sad.

"Where does the kid go?" he'd ask his wife, later. "You ask him a simple question and he takes twenty minutes to answer."

"I know," is all she would say, "I know."

His father felt the fault lay in the name, that if they had not named him Demetrius, but instead Joe or Sam for instance, the child might have been different—"normal," or at least, okay. But his wife's insistence on naming him after her great uncle who had "done well," had kept him silent on the subject. But now, looking at the boy, somewhat frail and already wearing glasses on that serious face—and especially recalling the fact that his son had dropped every ball he had tried to throw him over the years—he knew in his heart of hearts no other name would really fit. Certainly not Demy, the nickname he had tried calling him for awhile, to his wife's consternation.

Demetrius tended to stay in his room at night, long after his homework was finished, devouring one of the many books he brought home from the library. Or sometimes he would just sit with his eyes close to the fish bowl and watch the goldfish swim, imagining he was the fish and how it might feel to swim in the bowl and dart up to the top to retrieve the sprinkled food. Curiously, Demetrius had never given the fish a name.

One night he closed his eyes and imagined how it might feel to the fish to be let out into the ocean. He thought of the difference in water temperature, and the difference in the movement of the water. And when he thought of the current, his mind saw the fish being swept out with the undertow, way, way out, miles out, to a whole different world. Then Demetrius saw the goldfish going down, and further down still, as the water became colder, darker, and almost motionless. He saw seaweed moving with graceful abandon, as if waving, beckoning his little goldfish on to the mysterious "deep" he had read about in one of his books on the ocean.

Then his mind saw nothing but total darkness, as the goldfish neared the bottom of the ocean, the ocean floor. Suddenly, there were streaks and pockets of light given off by various colorful fish swimming by. Some flashed on and off, as if communicating.

"How beautiful!" he whispered to himself. And as one after another of unusual species of fish swam by in their fantastic shapes and neon-like colors, Demetrius said aloud, "Oh! . . . *Oh!*" Presently, his ears became so attuned to his imagination that the other-worldly quiet of the ocean deep enveloped him, and the light the different fish gave off began to increase—like the slow light over the dining room table, which his mother liked to turn up.

As he watched the little goldfish adjust to its new environment, he saw a curious baby seahorse poke at it with it's long nose. He saw them look at each other, and then slowly, begin to play. And Demetrius—himself an outsider—marveled at how wonderfully and naturally they played together, though so very different, wishing this were true for him. He followed their antics with joy for some minutes, until the little seahorse swam on.

Other, not so friendly-looking fish, floated by, but miraculously left the goldfish alone. An octopus came dangerously close, but only out of curiosity. Undulating jellyfish danced close, too, seemingly only to show themselves off. Then a small squid cut through the water within inches, but did no damage other than stirring up the cold water, which flipped the goldfish over once or twice.

Soon, as if wanting to go home, the goldfish began to swim

upwards. Demetrius, watching from below, could just barely make out the beginnings of the light above, which was streaming now from the sun, as the fish swam into it. His mind wondered, *Does moonlight pierce the water in a similar way?* But as soon as he had this thought, the ocean vanished.

He opened his eyes and saw his goldfish swimming happily in its own habitat.

Demetrius clicked off the room light and knelt down by the window, looking out at the full moon. Then he studied the long path made by moonlight on the grass in the yard until the yard became the surface of the ocean, lit by the moon. But suddenly the water turned turbulent and the moonlight faded. A boat appeared, riding huge, treacherous waves. *Such a fierce storm!* Demetrius marveled, as the intense sounds of wind, and the crashing of the sea filled his room. All at once, he felt spray from the sea on his arm, and began to see himself on the boat. He felt slightly woozy as the boat surged way up and then straight down, like a roller coaster, riding the gigantic waves.

"I'll ride it out!" he whispered, his eyes closed tight, his face tilted upward toward the night, his hair blowing straight back from the wind.

"I will!" The water was crashing now, over the deck, all about him.

Suddenly, he heard his mother's voice on the stairs, and was taken out of the dream.

"Goodness, his light is already out," she said, and added, "Maybe he was tired."

Then he heard his father's heavy footfalls on the steps.

"The boy doesn't know what tired is. Wait 'till he gets out in the real world."

"He knows what tired is," he heard his mother say. "His mind makes him tired."

Demetrius was still at the window long after he heard them enter their room. Long after the water stopped in their bathroom. Even after he began to hear their strange sounds. His father's grunts didn't stay with him, it was more his mother's strange, "Ah, ah, oh!" that penetrated his thoughts. As if she, somehow, were transported into a wonder similar to that his mind had imposed.

And then he imagined his mother going down, down, and further down, into the ocean, her hair floating out all around her. And the peaceful look on her face was one he had never seen before.

Rosa

Rosa Merriman did not come to full bloom until she was almost forty. It took that much time for her soft voice to get itself heard. And for her shy eyes to meet yours, steady on.

In the past, if she ventured a remark it was never before first considering how it might be taken. Especially among her husband's peers who taught at the same university and had received no less than eight prestigious awards among them, and all of whom came to their popular Friday night dinners. The fact that her own education was spotty—night school at three different universities—had cast a shadow, though there had been subsequent years of heavy, eclectic reading.

Often, listening to the voices rising and falling around the table, she would find herself tapping her foot impatiently and thinking, *Cut to the chase! Don't go around the world on this one!* And though she wanted to—and more, though she had read and come to her own conclusions on much of what was discussed—she never interrupted. Nor did her husband, Arthur, in deference to her shyness, encourage her to join in.

But one Friday night frustration got the best of her and her opinions were thrown out without even a glance as to their effect, and that shadow which had long held her back, lifted. Her natural instinct for the bottom line of things stood out sharp and clear in that room full of pontificating pundits.

The illustrious group around the dinner table put down their forks, did not know what to think, it was all so sudden. Before, her quietness only caused them to assume she was agreeing, or simply had no opinion. But now, hearing the new Rosa state her long held-in thoughts, they were shocked. She argued with them, even! Sweet Rosa Merriman who had simply smiled quietly when some questionable politician was discussed, or cleared the table while the rest of them sat pondering the state of the world's ecology or the rise of spirituality in literature, awaiting their dessert. Now she didn't leave the table, rather looked them straight in the eye and let them know she did not agree at all. And while someone else brought the coffee and searched for a knife to cut the pie, she stated at least three or four well thought-out ideas, to back up her opinion.

Arthur just sat with his mouth open. And the heads, normally fixed on Arthur Merriman, slowly turned to Rosa. Their popular Friday night dinners took a decidedly different twist. Her name, almost never mentioned before, now seemed on everyone's tongue.

"Rosa . . . Rosa Merriman, Arthur's wife. You must meet her. A most original mind. Her ability to connect things will astound you."

And if anyone spotted her walking down a street or going into a store, they would say, "There goes Rosa Merriman!" and wave her over. Where in the past they might have simply nodded, and continued on with their conversations. Or, more often than not, been only aware of her on the periphery.

Totally chagrined at his loss of place, Arthur stayed downstairs after their soirées and secretly looked up whoever Rosa had quoted, always discovering she was right on target.

And when he finally did turn out the lights and step softly up the stairs, he found she was not only awake but waiting for him in new, seductive gowns. And the Rosa who put her arms around him now, did so with such feral abandon he felt as if he were having an affair.

Now he hurried them all home on Friday nights. Where they once had lingered over some exciting debate, he would say, "But it will all be the same tomorrow, will it not?" and go and get their coats.

Elroy McCree

Elroy was crazy about her. Especially when she was playing her guitar and making up songs. Times like that, he'd just watch her with a smile that kept growing. Until one morning when she sat looking out the window, one leg tucked under her white terry cloth robe, sipping coffee and strumming a cord or two, she suddenly turned and said, "El! You know what? Somebody ought to write a ballad about you."

"Why?"

"Your name . . . It's perfect for a ballad."

"I don't *want* a ballad made up about me," he told her.

But, ignoring this, she started strumming a totally different kind of rhythm than he was used to hearing her play. And from that moment, it was as if she left the flesh and blood Elroy McCree, for the one she was creating.

Pretty soon, the rhythm of the thing started getting on his nerves. And the hunt and peck method she used to choose various words that rhymed—which before he considered kind of cute—was now to him like chalk scraping slowly on a blackboard.

"This is going to give me my real break," she told him. "This is going to open doors for me."

But the truth was, he didn't want any doors opening for her. He was afraid she would leave him.

Up to that time, he had loved their long, lazy weekends together. Both worked hard during the week, she as a typist, and he as a welder in the shipyard. But when Friday night came and she brought her things over in a little suitcase, with her guitar strapped to her shoulder, they entered another world. Sometimes they would go out to eat or to a movie, or take long walks together, but the thing he loved most was just having her there—just her sweet *presence*. And those special Saturday mornings when she sat in the window seat, strumming and singing softly while he made pancakes, put a warm spot, right over his heart.

But now things had changed. And they got even worse. She started calling him Elroy, instead of El—the name she had given him when they first started going out.

"Let's get married," he said one Saturday morning, in the middle of her strumming.

"What?" she said, not looking at him, her fingers still playing with the chords.

"Married. Let's get married."

She stopped playing then, and looked over at him. "Now wouldn't be the best time," she told him.

Elroy had not planned to propose that morning, it just came out, partly to stop that incessant ballad rhythm. He wanted to marry her— it was always in the back of his mind—still it surprised him when he actually said the words. But now her reply surprised him more.

"Why wouldn't it?" he asked.

"I can't concentrate on anything but this ballad now, can't you see that? It's my big chance. Can't you see that, Elroy?"

"You used to call me El."

"I forget. But your name, after all, *is* Elroy."

"I like for you to call me El. I never liked the name Elroy, you know that. Never in my whole life."

"It's a great name. It's going to be a great song. Here, let me sing a little."

"I've *heard* it! I want us to get married."

"You've heard only bits and pieces. I've just about got it now. It's almost there . . . "

She picked up the guitar again and began singing, but this time as if she were singing in a night club, or on a big city stage. And where she had once sat looking out the window, strumming and singing softly, she now sang out clear and full voiced, looking straight at him as if he were a real audience.

Elroy was amazed. He had never seen this side of her, before. At first, he didn't even hear the words, he was too shocked by the sheer

11

talent unfolding right before him. And the more self assurance she displayed as she sang, the more insecure he felt. He started listening, really listening, to the words. The song seemed all about a man named Elroy McCree, and how somebody stole his girl and took her away to New York City, "where millions of lights made things look pretty." The song went on:

"But Elroy McCree set out that night,
To the big city, to make things right.
He looked in Chinatown and all around,
But never did see his girl.
He got lost in Brooklyn and scared in Queens,
Got held up in a subway by a gang that was mean.
But never did see his girl.
He wandered and walked and looked all around,
But the love of his life was not to be found.
He never did see his girl.
Poor Elroy McCree. Poor Elroy McCree.
He never did see his girl."

When she stopped singing, the electricity was still in the room.

"Well . . . what do you think?" she said, eyes still lit, her voice as energized as a plucked cord.

He was still somewhat in shock. He didn't quite know what to say. "I never wanted my name in any ballad," he said finally.

She looked at him for a full minute with her forehead screwed up. Then darted out of the room.

He thought at first she was crying, and in a moment went to the door of the bedroom.

"I'm sorry," he said through the door, but it was already too late. She was throwing her things into the little suitcase.

About two years later, he read about the success of the ballad, and how somebody had even written a musical based on it. That fall, he went to New York to hear her sing on stage—she was in that musical—but when he tried to see her, he couldn't get near her for the fans.

He found himself walking around Chinatown in a daze. All of a sudden, he stopped. It was then he wondered which came first, the song or this happening. And it seemed to him that life was past, present and future, all jumbled up together.

"We only thought it was one, two, three," he said out loud.

Later, he tried to call her, but then put down the phone. It was no use. He had no desire to see the singer. The one he wanted to see was the sweet, soft-spoken girl she had been before.

In the morning, in an airplane high in the sky heading home, Elroy McCree looked out the window. The sun, just now rising, lit up the clouds with color, but mumbling to himself, he barely noticed.

"You wouldn't think a man's name would do him in," he said.

It seemed the success of the ballad just wouldn't die down. Though she had written other songs, and even now had her own CDs, it was always "Elroy McCree" they wanted to hear.

"Elroy McCree!" they yelled. "Sing about Elroy!" It kept his memory uppermost in her mind. And often when she was singing the ballad she got teary.

After one concert, she called him. "El," she said, "fame isn't all it's cracked up to be."

And shortly after that they were married.

It wasn't easy. She had long stints on the road, but always came back to him. And sometimes Elroy went with her, sitting up front at the concerts, still trying to get used to that electrifying voice—always asking himself how someone like *that* could want somebody like him.

Clay

Clay Copeland's life was pretty much under control, until that day at the airport. He had a layover between planes, and had got up to stretch his legs a moment and people watch. When a man walked by wearing a tee shirt with the words "Final Answer" on the front, Clay turned to see what words might follow on the back, and there she was, as if she, herself, were the answer, looking straight at him.

She smiled and he smiled back, and she walked toward him like a relative or spouse about to make contact after a very long time.

"Reggie," she said, her arms out, "I've missed you so much."

"I'm not . . ."

"It's all right," she said, hugging him now, "You don't have to explain."

"Really, I'm . . ." he said, pulling back.

"No! Don't say it! Don't say a word. It's all my fault," she said, putting her soft hand over his mouth.

Those eyes were incredible, he thought. A kind of green he had never seen.

"I should never have said those things to you." The green eyes clouded; one tear fell down her cheek.

What was happening, he thought. Did he have a double? What!

"Please," he said to her, ". . . you must listen."

But she just put her head on his shoulder and wept, and all he could do was hold her. The blonde hair, just under his chin, was soft and smelled of jasmine.

"There has been a mistake," he said, trying to disentangle himself.

"The whole thing was a mistake!" she cried, grabbing his lapels. "I'm so very, very sorry," she said into his jacket.

You would think I was cloned! he thought. He looked over her head and quickly scanned the people still waiting for someone—a family of four, an old couple, and a woman, but no possible Reggie. He pulled away now, took her by the shoulders and positioned her a safe distance.

"I am not Reggie," he told her in a firm voice.

"What are you talking about?"

"You are mistaken. I am not the man you think."

She looked at him closely, her mouth slightly open. Her pink lipstick had a high sheen.

"Is this your way of punishing me?" she said, trying to compose herself now.

"My name is Clay Copeland," he said, and this time his voice was definite.

"My God, Reggie, don't you ever tire of acting," she said. "What is it now—you got the part you wanted, right? Couldn't you have waited to tell me?" She shook her head in disbelief. "Don't you realize this is not a time for one of your games?" There was a deep sadness in the words.

"I need to get my suitcase," she said, looking away from him now.

"I don't know how to make you understand," he said.

"No, you never did! And to think I apologized to you. Apologized!" And with that, she turned and walked briskly away.

He looked at his watch. His plane was due in exactly twenty-five minutes. "Damn," he whispered.

By the time he got to the baggage claim area, he thought he'd missed her. But there she stood, a look of resignation on her face, watching the suitcases go around and around, as if hypnotized. As disturbed as he was at the whole encounter, he could not help noticing those perfect legs.

When he saw her pulling an obviously heavy bag off the turn, he started over. Before he got there she already had it off, and was trying to read the tag with big glasses, leaning down quite close. He watched her slip the glasses back into her purse and start to pick up the suitcase again.

"Let me do that," he said, taking the suitcase. He could at least carry it as far as the big doors, he thought.

"I am not going with you," she said, her voice elevated. "You've played your last game on me!"

People were staring at them. One elderly woman, in particular, gave him a hard frown.

He took her elbow and steered her away, a short distance from the crowd.

"Look," he said, putting down the suitcase, "I don't know what your situation is, but you have absolutely got to believe me when I tell you I am not the person you think I am."

"That is so low, Reggie, so low."

"Here," he said, taking out his drivers' license and handing it to her.

"My name is Clay Copeland. I'm a computer programmer," he told her, taking out another card and holding it up for her to see.

"And I'm single," he added, though not knowing why he threw that in.

She squinted at the drivers' license, then back at him. "You have never gone this far. A fake license!" The incredible eyes turned to cold, green steel. "You are despicable!" she hissed. Then she threw the card as far as she could.

He ran to retrieve the card, and when he looked up again he saw her walking out the big airport doors, the suitcase banging at her side.

He glanced at his watch; if he hurried he could just make his plane. He hesitated for only a moment, staring at the doors and biting his lower lip. Then he turned and started walking quickly away. He brushed by the same elderly lady, who he was sure must have observed the whole thing—her mouth was still open.

"I'm not Reggie," he said to her, hurrying on, wishing so very much at that moment that he were.

He was the last person to board the plane. Still breathless, he adjusted the seat belt and tried to relax. He felt, oddly, as if he had lost his best friend. He traced a cloud beyond the window with his finger, and sighed. When he remembered she had not worn a wedding ring, he sighed again.

Then he sat up straight, thinking of the suitcase and the name on that tag. M.K. something. Or was it N.K. something? The stewardess was working her way down the aisle, taking orders.

"Thompson!" he said aloud, finally. "That's it!" Two people in the seats directly opposite, craned their necks and stared. He gave them a maniacal smile, then searched for his pen to write the name down. I'll find her! he thought.

After all, he told himself when he put the pen away, looking back toward the window with a sly smile, old Reggie didn't stand a chance now.

Stormi

It was a handle she hated. And she had carried it twenty-four years. In all that time, there was not one man she had met who had not made some distasteful comment about it.

Just last week she reluctantly accepted a blind date with a friend's cousin, and at first, was so pleasantly surprised she even thought he might be "the one." But after dinner when they rose to dance he held her much too tight and whispered, "Your name . . . is it indicative of some steamy passion?" She looked him straight in the eye and answered in a voice now turned cool, "Quite the opposite."

She often wondered about people who lived into their names. Like Sally Ride, for instance, the first woman to ride in a space ship, or the minister, John Church, or any number of other people whose lives reflected their names. And occasionally, she daydreamed about what would happen if she lived into hers. Being of a spontaneous nature, one day the idea took hold. *Just to see what it might feel like,* she told herself. *Just for a few days.* And that's how she ended up taking a short vacation in a city where she did not know a living soul.

After she got to Seattle, she applied right away for a job as a dancer by answering an ad she saw in the paper. When she checked out the address with the hotel manager, he raised his eyebrows. "The Finale Club?" he asked. "I don't think you want to go *there*," he said, "It's a club that caters to the military . . . mostly men." Her question had clarified his conviction that most tourists had absolutely no idea about anything. And his answer told her that she had picked the right club.

The interview, or "audition," was set up for the next day. She didn't think it would be a problem; she had taken dance lessons all her life. *Just improvise*, she told herself.

She practiced in the big mirror on the back of the hotel door, imagining she was maneuvering a slow hula hoop with her hips. If she exaggerated that movement—almost like making a caricature of it—it might work, she thought. They would bill her as Stormi, of course. When she saw this in her mind's eye, she laughed out loud.

While she practiced, she thought again of her mother's answer when she had asked many years ago, why in the world they named her Stormi. She never received an adequate reply, only "We just thought it was cute, and seemed to match that fiery red hair of yours."

When the time came for the interview, she felt she had the routine down pat. At three o'clock she pushed open the door of the Finale Club, and ventured into the dark foyer. After her eyes got adjusted to the shadows, she asked the faded cheerleader type behind the counter where she might find Mr. Landell.

"Stormi, right?"

She nodded.

"You'll need to fill this out, first."

After Stormi filled out the application, the girl took it upstairs. It seemed she was gone a long time. Waiting uncomfortably on a bar stool, Stormi glanced around. Three men sat at the end of the bar; one winked. She took out a little notebook from her pocketbook and pretended to write.

When the girl came back, she said, "His office is upstairs. First door on the left."

As Stormi walked up the steps, she saw they were in need of vacuuming, then noted a large, badly painted picture of a nude on the adjoining wall. When she reached the first door on the left—it was half open—she put one finger on it tentatively, and pushed.

"Mr. Landell?" she said to the big man hovering over some papers.

He looked up, then down, all the way down to her toes. "That's me," he said.

"Well . . . I'm . . . Stormi."

"Take a seat," he told her, gesturing with his cigar. And after she sat down, he said, chewing on the end of the cigar, "I've been looking over your application." Then his voice turned curt.

"Why do you want this?" he said. "Are you working for the police?"

She half-laughed. "No!"

Your experience does not exactly match your desire, here," he told her, tapping the paper.

She had fabricated all of it, but realized now she must have made the application sound too normal, anyway.

"Look, Mr. Landell . . . I'll be honest. I've never danced in a club like this before, but I'd like to see if I can. You know? I like to dance . . . I really do."

"Yeah, sure."

"No, I really do. And I'm good. I think. Anyway, can't you just watch me for five minutes?"

Landell studied her question a moment, smiled slow, then got up.

"Okay, lady . . . let's see what you got."

He led her back downstairs and started the music—the kind they used when the band was not playing.

She took off her skirt—a wrap-around—and walked up the stage steps in her short shorts. When she got the feel of the music, she eased into it. After about a minute or so, Landell motioned to someone who put a spotlight on her, then motioned to someone else who immediately manned the drums and began whisking the snare around and around to the music.

"Get into it," Landell said. Then, after a moment, "Good . . . Good!"

When she finished, she pushed her red hair back, out of her face, and waited. Then shielded her eyes from the harsh light and looked out to the nearest table, which was enclosed in a tent of cigar smoke.

"Not bad," the voice from the table said. "You can start tonight."

The girl out front was instructed to get a costume for Stormi.

"The green and gold," Landell told her.

When the girl brought the costume back and handed it to Stormi, she said, "It should fit. It stretches." Then pointed to a room down the hall. "You can try it on in there."

Stormi looked at the box. There was no way she was going to try the outfit on until it was thoroughly cleaned. "I'll need to take it home and try it, she told the girl. I'm in a big hurry." And before the girl could protest, Stormi was out the door.

I can't believe I'm doing this, she said to herself. And continued to repeat that all the way back to the hotel. And when she opened the box and took out the costume, she laughed so hard she fell back on the bed.

After she composed herself, she washed the outfit three times, and then put it in the hotel dryer on the lowest possible setting, opening the door a couple of times to see that the tassels did not fall off as it went around.

Back in her room, Stormi put the shiny little costume on, and looked at herself in the mirror. The green and gold reminded her of her high school colors and the outfit she had worn as a drum majorette. Except, she thought, that outfit would make six of the one she now had on.

She tried a few exaggerated hula hoop movements, even adding the touch of pushing her long hair up, and letting it fall from her fingers. Then she started giggling, wondering what her co-workers at Harris and Fine—where she was a CPA—would think. And immediately fell back on the bed again, laughing. *How on* earth *will I do this with a straight face?* she asked herself.

That night, she stood at the curtain, waiting for the band's drum roll as she had been told. It reminded her a little of ballet recitals, when she had waited in the wings, at age twelve. Only this was a far cry from *The Nutcracker Suite.*

She heard the MC introduce her as *"Stormi . . . the new sensation . . . fresh from Memphis!"* She had never even been to Memphis, and had to suppress a giggle that she hoped would not escalate.

When the drum roll started, the MC added, *Come on out, Stormi . . . Bring us a little of that special electricity!* She bit her tongue to suppress hysteria, and walked on out, into the bright lights.

Afterward, she had a note from Landell.

"Some important gentlemen are at my table and want to meet you."

She turned the paper over and wrote, "Sorry. I need to get home," and slipped out the back way, and into a taxi. One more time, she told herself, and that's it.

The next night, as soon as she arrived, one of the girls took her aside.

"Mr. Landell wants you to add this step to your routine," she said, and began moving her body in a way that left nothing, absolutely nothing to the imagination.

"I'm not going to do *that!*" Stormi told her.

The girl just shrugged her shoulders, and walked away.

This isn't funny anymore, Stormi thought, and walked up the creaky steps to Landell's office.

"I'm not adding that step to my routine," she told him.

"Stormi . . . Stormi . . . it's a minor thing. You've got a great body, you know. Show it off!"

"I'm quitting"

"What?"

"Quitting."

Landell drummed the fingers of his left hand on the desk. The diamond on his pinky flashed.

"Okay . . . so don't add the step," he told her.

"It's not just that."

He looked at her hard.

"I just wanted to see if I could do it, that's all. Well, I've done it."

"You realize I can't pay you, if you don't go on tonight."

"Yes."

"Look lady . . . go on tonight. Then you'll get paid. Otherwise," he said narrowing his eyes, "You'll get a big, fat zero for *both* nights."

She looked at him just as hard.

"I'll take the big, fat zero," she told him, and walked out.

The experiment was a huge flop, she said to herself, packing up. Not the "fun" thing she had envisioned at all. *Seedy* was the only description that came to mind. *What on earth had* possessed her!

When she got back home, she changed her name to Sharon. The legalities were a lot of trouble, but people tended to get used to the name after a while. And the ones who didn't—well, she moved on.

She found the men she met now, responded to the name Sharon in a totally different way. Right off there was more respect. She found herself even toning down her makeup, going for more subtle clothes—walking a little different. And for the first time in her life, she felt she was the woman she was meant to be. She wished she had changed her name years ago.

She never told anybody about the trip to Seattle. Though she was tempted years later, when her husband, Jim—whom she had met after changing her name to Sharon—made a comment that something she was wearing looked "a little too prim."

Blessing

"My little blessing," her mother had whispered in the hospital that rainy night she came into the world. And as if to prove it, her mother wrote BLESSING as clear as you please, when they asked for the child's name.

Blessing perceived early on that there was something special about her name. At the family reunion, when she saw great Aunt Thelma looking sad—she had just lost Uncle Melvin—Blessing put a cookie into her blue-veined hand, then laid her head on Thelma's arm.

"She truly is our little blessing!" they all said. And Blessing found as long as she stayed "sweet," as they were wont to call her, she met everyone's expectations. She offered to help and smiled a lot, and often this brought gifts and privileges the other children did not know existed. Even when she was a teenager and all her classmates were giving their parents fits, she somehow contained her hormones and continued to smile. And as she got older, she was the one they all called on, when something was needed. They knew they could count on their Blessing.

But when Eddie came along, things changed. Only six months after they were married they began having problems.

"You might have been your mama's, but you sure as hell are no blessing to me." That was usually after he asked her to do something, and she—for no apparent reason—just plain wouldn't.

"Why in the devil you knock yourself out for everybody else but when it comes to me, you can't even bring home a simple bag of pretzels when you know how much I love pretzels!"

Once he even told her, "Your mama was crazy. You're no blessing. You come straight from hell!" That was after she threw out his old fishing jacket.

"My favorite one!" The fact that she said it stunk to high heaven didn't make a bit of difference.

The trouble was, she could only be herself with him. All those years of being nice, of pleasing everybody, had caused a well of pent-up emotions and now she was taking all that pent-up aggravation out on him. Too, the fact that his job transfer landed them 800 miles away from family seemed to unleash something feral in her.

He couldn't understand it. All he knew was that she was not the person he married. Not the sweet Blessing he had courted.

At first, it was funny. He would almost tease her into an argument, just to see the fire in her eyes. And after a good fight, they would tumble into bed, and the feistiness in her just enhanced the whole thing. Afterward, you couldn't get a toothpick between them.

But pretty soon, she would end up vexing him all over again.

Once he came home from work and before he even got the key halfway in the door, she jerked it open and yelled,

"You didn't do it!"

"Do what?" he said.

"Take the trash out! And you knew it was Tuesday!"

When he had to give her name to his boss for insurance purposes, his boss said, "Blessing? What kind of name is that?"

And Eddie just shrugged and said, "A bat out of hell name, that's what."

He took to calling her B.L. a combination of Blessing and her middle name, Louise. In his mind, it sure fit better than Blessing.

When they went back south to see her family, the old Blessing came to the fore. Eddie just sat in awe of the transformation. People said he had grown quiet since the marriage. Actually, he was dumbfounded.

But, still, after a couple of years and several trips back south to see her family, he found—oddly enough—he liked her better when she was her real self.

He never regretted their not being able to have children. The very thought that there could have been two Blessings under one roof, made him tremble. Too, as time went by, there was something complete about their union that seemed to need no other stimulus.

But if their early years had been tumultuous, the first year of Blessing's menopause topped it all.

One night Eddie put the paper down and said, "B.L., I'm freezing. What's happened to the heat?"

She was hemming a dress. "There's nothing wrong with the heat."

He got up and checked the thermostat, then yelled from the hall, "Sixty-two degrees!"

"Don't you change that thing. I finally got the temperature right in here."

"It's winter time! And we are living in New England, not on a tropical isle!

"I don't care if we are living on the moon, the temperature is just fine."

He got so he would simply get up from whatever they were doing—watching TV mostly—and sneak into the hall and push the thermostat up.

But then she'd start fanning herself or turn a little red in the face, and he found out right quick it didn't add to her disposition a bit to keep the heat up too high. He simply left it alone and put on more sweaters.

He had hated the cold, ever since they moved to Vermont—especially hated shoveling all that snow. But she actually thrived on everything about the area. Eddie thought it was mainly because she could be as ornery as she wanted and nobody even noticed. In fact, to his mind she fit right in.

Another time, he said, "B.L. what is the matter with you today?"

"I've got AMS."

"What?"

"I've got AMS!" she yelled. "Can't you hear!"

"What in hell is AMS?"

"After Menses Syndrome. AMS! AMS! AMS!"

"I heard you!"

Later, Eddie slipped out and drove down to the drugstore. When he saw that all the people in the druggist corner had cleared out, he walked over.

"What do you have for AMS?" he asked the druggist.

"For what?"

"AMS. You know, After Menses Syndrome."

The druggist had not had a good day. Every conceivable possible thing that could go wrong had.

"I don't know what you are talking about," he told Eddie.

"AMS . . . AMS! AMS!"

"Look, you are going to have to be a little more specific, here."

Eddie was not about to go home without something in his hand to calm a wild woman.

"The thing women get . . . you know. You *should* know."

The druggist was looking just beyond Eddie's head, at the clock on the wall. He had only ten more minutes to put up with these people.

"It's PMS." he told Eddie. "PMS."

"No! Not PMS . . . AMS!"

"There is no AMS," the druggist said disinterestedly.

"Women get it!"

"There is nothing for AMS," the druggist said, examining his nails.

"There sure as hell better be!"

The druggist looked Eddie straight in the eye.

"Look for yourself," he told him, and as he moved away from the counter added, "Aisle four."

Eddie walked over to aisle four, muttering to himself. He stood there for some minutes, looking over the section containing Midol, Tampax, and things of that order. He was down to the shelf that contained douches when an announcement on the loud speaker informed that the store was closing.

"Well . . . if that don't beat all," he said out loud, and stomped out the door.

After he retired he started fishing regularly, mainly to get out of the house. But when the novelty wore off, he found himself telling the guys goodbye early and heading back home to see what B.L. was up to.

Once she went home to see her family, by herself. It was the first time they had ever really been separated, and the first few quiet hours in the house were bliss to Eddie. He did everything he knew would irritate her if she had been there. And every time he went by the thermostat in the hall, he moved it up or down—just for the sheer joy of it. But that night when he turned over in his sleep and threw his arm out and felt nothing but an empty space, it woke him so definitively that he decided he might as well get up. Before he turned on the light, he looked out the window at the snow falling in a slant against the streetlight. So many nights they had lain in each other's arms and watched the snow fall against that light. It was as if, after all these years, that silent snow had seduced him. And he had learned to love it.

But the snow now magnified the quiet house, and the loud creaking on the steps as he went downstairs, and the sudden dong of the grandfather's clock, startled. By that night he no longer enjoyed changing the thermostat, and he had to admit he really missed her.

"Come home soon," he said to her on the phone, "I miss you, hon."

"I miss you, too, sweetheart," the old Blessing said, mellowed from being around her relatives. The voice was too sweet—he was about to lose the feeling until she added, "Did you remember to fix that washing machine?"

"Not yet," he told her.

"Not yet! What are you waiting for . . . the thing to fix itself! I *told* you ninety times . . . "

He stopped her right there, his smile spreading.

"Get on home, B.L."

Arabella

There was a rhythm in Arabella's name. When her mother called her in from play, it was as if she were singing. "Araaa BEL-la," she would call out, and the child would come skipping up the back steps like a dancer.

In fact, all of Arabella's movements were those of a dancer. Even when photographed, her little fingers would pose like a ballerina. And when she walked down the long stairway at home, she appeared to her family more to float. "A natural grace," her father declared and they enrolled her in ballet school, which she took to immediately.

She remained thin, with light, airy movements which delighted her ballet teacher and made her first choice as a partner for all the boys in her class. It was not until later, after she married Charles, a young lawyer, that she began to put on a little weight for the first time. It made her linger at the long mirror with alarm at first—then with awe, when she found she was pregnant.

After the baby was born Arabella never quite went back to her original size, although the wispiness, the lightness, remained. And always, always, she floated down stairs. Once, Charles stood at the bottom of the steps looking up as she descended the stairway in a new chiffon dress looking willowy and ethereal, and he almost put his arms out to catch her.

The baby looked just like Arabella, and was the center of her life. Charles named him Aaron, liking the "strong sound of it."

As the boy grew, it soon became apparent that he had much the same wispiness as his mother. And when she began to teach dancing—taking him along to watch—he began to mimic the dancers. Arabella thought it "cute." Charles, being treated to these antics at home, thought it appalling.

"Get a sitter," he told her. "The boy doesn't need to go with you."

But she continued to take him, sensing in the child a real talent for dance—the way his eyes shut and his body swayed to the music, the way he tried to follow the dancers at the bar. Arabella even had a special little bar added, just for him.

"It will be our secret," she told the boy, "Daddy doesn't need to know."

Some years later, as Aaron was just about to enter high school, Charles noticed ballet shoes in his closet and exploded. "The boy is sissy enough! He doesn't need ballet shoes to prove it!" Charles was still sorely disappointed that Aaron did not share his strong interest in sports.

"He's good," Arabella said simply. "He has talent."

"Oh, God."

"There's no mistaking it. And it *could* be . . . a major talent."

"Oh, my God."

One morning, as Charles was putting on his jacket to leave for work he saw his son begin to descend the stairs, and stopped, with only one arm in the jacket, and watched with his mouth open. The boy was floating—much the same as his mother—barely touching the steps, his hand brushing the top of the banister with only the slightest, intermittent contact.

"Morning, Dad," the boy said, and walked on past him, to the dining room.

"Yes. . . ." Charles answered absently, his mind still on the spectacle.

Charles' fears about his son became paramount when Aaron went off to college. Then became reality when Aaron quit in the third year and went to New York to dance, and met Simon.

When Aaron brought Simon home one weekend, all their lives changed. Arabella welcomed Simon into their house as she would any friend of Aaron's. But Charles maintained a steely reserve.

Saturday morning, when he heard their voices outside, Charles put down his paper and went to the window. He watched them going down the walkway with their tennis rackets, laughing, Aaron's arm lightly hooked on Simon's shoulder. Something about the familiarity of that arm destroyed Charles' last hope.

Arabella came and stood beside Charles at the window. "They are very close," she said.

"Any fool can see that."

"Simon seems a nice young man."

Charles walked away from the window and took up his paper. "You two certainly got on. One would think you were about to adopt him!" He jerked the paper open and pretended to read.

"We are going to have to accept our son's lifestyle, sooner or later."

He moved his face around the paper and looked at her.

"No, *you* might accept it. I never will!"

"He's your son. Your only son."

"That doesn't change anything."

Taking a deep breath first, she said, "The ballet is in two weeks, and he wants us to come."

Charles put down the paper and looked straight at her.

"You know how hard he has worked for this," she said. "It would mean *so* much to him."

"Under *no* circumstances will I go to New York to see my son *prancing* on a stage." And as if she might not have heard him, he repeated, "*No* circumstances!"

"You are going to lose him, you know," she said softly and left the room.

On Sunday, just before they left, Aaron opened the door to the study. "Dad," he began. Charles took his glasses off and lowered his book.

". . . we're going, now."

When Charles remained quiet, Aaron came into the room and sat down.

"What do you think of Simon?" he asked in a serious voice.

"I don't know, Aaron. I don't really know your friend very well."

"Well, whose fault is that? We've hardly seen you all weekend."

"I've been busy . . . working on something for Tilly."

Aaron didn't believe this for a minute. Mr. Tilly was the other partner in his dad's law firm, and Aaron had known the man since he was a small boy. If anything, Tilly would have been working on something for Charles.

"Simon is more than a friend, Dad. You might as well know that."

"I guessed as much," Charles said, looking away.

"He's . . . a very special person. I wish you had taken the time to get to know him. I think you'd like him."

"I can tell you right now, I'm *never* going to like your lifestyle . . . or *anybody that's a part of it,*" Charles said. Then, jabbing the air with one finger for emphasis, he added. "So get that straight."

Aaron looked at his father hard. "I got it," he said. Then left the room.

From the window, Charles watched the two boys pack up the car. Even watched Arabella float down the steps and take them both in her arms.

When the car sped off, he went downstairs, but not for dinner. He told Arabella he was not hungry, then put on his jacket and walked out the front door.

A half hour later he was on his second drink at Michael's, a neighborhood bar, when Arabella slid into the seat beside him.

"Was it that bad for you?" she said in a tired voice.

"My son is gay. Yes, it was that bad for me."

"He's going to have a lot of people against him, Charles. He doesn't need us against him, as well."

"Arabella, I can't alter my feelings here. I cannot condone this."

"He can't change, you must know that."

"He doesn't *want* to change."

"No . . . he can't change. None of them can."

"Well they can all go to hell as far as I'm concerned."

Arabella went to New York alone, to see their son perform with one of the finest ballet companies in the country. The standing ovation at the end was partially for Aaron, and brought tears to her eyes.

The reviews were spectacular. Arabella sent several to Charles, along with a note saying she had decided to remain in New York for a while. Later on, she left the hotel and went to stay with a cousin in Larchmont, coming into the city often to have dinner with Aaron and Simon, or to shop or see a play.

Charles wanted to know when she planned to return and she told him she really had not decided. He said maybe he would come up, but she said, no, the separation was probably doing them both good. He said to hell with it. But as the weeks went by, the house became more and more lonely, until one Saturday morning he slammed the front door behind him and headed for the airport.

At first, Arabella, though surprised, was glad to see him. But later, after they had spent some time together, she brought up the subject of Aaron and the negative tone in Charles' voice threatened to put back the distance between them. "Just try," she told him, whispering in his ear. He rubbed his mouth on her shoulder. They had been in bed the better part of the afternoon and the sun was just beginning to go down. He had missed her scent; he put his face between her breasts and breathed in. "Just try," she whispered, her voice faint now.

Afterward, they lay still, her head on his shoulder, both partially rose colored with the last of the sun's rays. She suggested they call Aaron, and Charles immediately turned away from her and bunched the pillow up under his arm. Arabella looked at his back, so solid and muscular. It was this, his solidity, that she had been drawn to when she married him; it anchored her. But now, in her heart of hearts she knew he was not going to call their son, nor—in all likelihood—see him. And in that moment the distance between them became concrete.

Almost two years later Arabella was still in New York, now teaching ballet. Aaron and Simon had bought a townhouse, and were happily decorating. Simon had just been promoted to senior editor of a large publishing company.

Charles never sent a letter to Aaron, nor received one.

Arabella had written Charles a considerable number of letters during their separation, which had dwindled to an occasional card. Now she was writing a final letter, telling him she had met someone and wanted a divorce.

"*He thinks like I do,* she said, then added, *His mind goes into the same paths.*"

That cold New York morning when she raised the letter up to the mail slot, there was a pause. She looked away; stores were already decorating for Christmas, and seeing this made the mailing even harder. After a long moment she took a deep breath, pushed the envelope into the slot, and walked quickly down the street, her eyes down, her coat collar up against the wind.

When the housekeeper brought the mail in and laid it on the end table beside Charles, she told him she had left his dinner on the warming tray, and was now going home. After the door shut behind her, Charles began to sort through the mail, stopping at once when he saw Arabella's handwriting.

He read the letter over and over again. Then just sat for a long time with a stoic expression, never realizing that in all his strong desire to see his son different, it was really he, himself, who could not change.

"To hell with them all," he said finally.

Burl

His daddy was the first in our county to own one, although it was not until he had already run off from Burl's mother and was living down the road with a blonde widow.

Of all the children, Burl was the only one who kept in contact—that dark brown Cadillac luring him down the road over and over again. Not that he ever got to drive it. Still, he'd love to run his hands over the smooth lines of it, and peer in the window at the plush-looking seats and the fancy controls.

His daddy, part salesman, mostly farmer, was a mystery to folks in the area since nobody knew where he got the money for that sort of car. I heard snide remarks, but tried not to pay too much attention because Burl was my best friend. I think it was partly this mystery of the car, and partly that Burl was the youngest and really missed the man, that caused him to slip out in the evenings, holding the screen door ever so careful to keep it from squeaking, and run quick down that dusty road, the only light coming from the moon and an occasional firefly.

But whenever Burl's mother found out where he had been, she whipped him good—until he got so big she just gave up.

Burl's daddy died late one fall and the blonde widow inherited the car, and that was that.

Afterwards, Burl moved sixty miles away and went to work in the same shoe factory that employed me. Before long, there were only two things in life he desired: to own a Cadillac, and to make enough money to buy out the factory and fire the boss.

His gift for gab proved even better than his daddy's, and when he discovered this for himself, he left the shoe factory and got into sales with a company out West. Slow moving by nature, I decided to stay on. Besides, I believed Burl's story of buying the place out someday.

Burl made some big money in sales, and he saved it. In the winter of '42, he took his wife of ten years down south for a visit, wrote out a whopping check, and signed the papers for the factory. Then he started looking for the foreman, Reet Burger.

I was there that day, working just across the aisle. Reet was in the middle of repairing a stalled machine when Burl walked up—cool as you please—and said, "You're fired."

When Reet's mouth hung open, Burl said, "I mean it . . . this is no joke."

After that, there was no place for Burl to go but up.

The factory grew to almost twice the business as before, and things were real pleasant now that Reet Burger was gone. Burl had only a ninth grade education, but something else had got in there somehow, and he seemed to be able to figure things the rest of us had no idea of—especially things to do with business and making money.

But one spring day—just like his daddy—Burl upped and left his wife without a word, and ran off with the young secretary he was long used to kidding with in the office, named Irene. I had been in Mavis and Burl's wedding and didn't much like to see him run off like he did, much less with someone who looked like his daughter. But I didn't say anything.

Soon afterwards, he left me in charge, then moved permanently to Florida.

I missed him, but we kept in touch through the factory. And sometimes Burl would pick up the telephone and call me, and not even talk business the whole time.

In the early days, Ellie and I would always stop by on our way to Daytona Beach, and surprise him. He'd say, "Come on in this house!" when he saw us at the door. Times like that, he seemed to pat me on the back forever. Before we left, we'd have to take a ride in his car—always the latest model, always a Cadillac—and he would push every one of the buttons, laughing and making us go up and down in our seats, or to lean backwards and forwards.

The last one was after Burl had sold the factory, and we were both retired. It was dark blue, and the computerized controls caused both Ellie and me to go quiet when Burl pointed out what this, and this, and that did. He seemed to hesitate, though, as if he was not quite sure himself what to expect. The fun seemed out of it now.

Then we noticed he had stopped putting his name, Burl T. Grover, on the dash (he used to have that done with gold lettering each time he bought a new car). I figured it was just too much with all those new controls, but Ellie said no, she thought he just didn't care anymore, like he used to.

When Irene called us about the funeral, we drove all the way from Texas, the longest trip I ever made, dream-like, really. Ellie had to ask me over and over again to slow down. It was like I had to hurry and get there and see for myself, to believe it.

We got there the day before, and I went straight to the funeral home. Looking down into that casket, I said to myself I needn't have hurried, Burl wasn't going anywhere. And I couldn't get over how much he looked like his daddy.

Some other fellow was driving around the Cadillac, picking up relatives from the airport and things like that. I noticed that often Irene went along.

Once when they left the house, the little handful of people sitting in the living room with us got real quiet. Finally, someone—a neighbor from next door—said, "He's gonna ruin that car, driving it so fast like he does," and several other people nodded. Ellie and I just looked at each other and raised shoulders.

Later, Irene told us he lived down the street, and had been "just real helpful while Burl was in the wheelchair and all." His name was Ken something or other.

The day of the funeral, Ken came over to drive Irene and Burl's grieving sister to the graveside service at the cemetery. The rest of us followed, or tried to follow as best we could, behind that careening Cadillac. Ellie said we wouldn't be in such a hurry, if Irene didn't always have to make up like a Barbie doll.

I saw Irene's face change when we got there.

"This isn't . . . it's not the right . . . ." she said with a pinched look. And right there, while everyone took their seats under the tent, she put her hands on her hips and stared fire at the casket.

I watched a thin man with thick, white hair rush over to her, and Ellie elbowed me in the ribs to say it was the funeral director. Then we heard them. She sure didn't lower her voice.

"It's not what you told me," she said to him. "It's not here . . ." Then she pointed to a lot under an oak tree, near the fence. "THERE!" she said, her finger quivering with anger.

The funeral director took her hand and looped it into the circle he made with his arm, and patted it.

"Well, we made a little mistake," he said, still patting. "But we can't change it now, can we? What we'll do," he said, putting his head down close to hers and trying to lower his voice, "is to go on and have the funeral . . . then later on I'll have it changed to the other lot. Just like you wanted it."

She jerked her arm out of the circle and looked him hard in the eye.

"There just better not be anything else!"

"No, no," he said softly. "Everything else is just fine." He took her hand again.

"Shall we go?" he asked, steering her towards the shaded area where we all sat under the green and white tent, waiting.

I almost felt the humor in the thing. Back in his good days, Burl would have laughed harder than anybody. He would have seen the joke in it, right quick—especially if it happened to somebody else.

But when the preacher's voice began, and a breeze started up, I felt the most awful loneliness. I tried to look away, toward the oak trees, but that only made it worse. And it wasn't just that I would miss old Burl, but that I knew it was only a matter of time before I would be in a box, too. I felt lonely for myself, missing the part of me that was already gone, even.

The breeze was the sweetest summer breeze I could remember in years, causing an occasional ripple and soft flapping in the scalloped overhang of the tent. That, and the buzzing of a nearby June bug, took me straight back to a summer when Burl and I sat barefoot around a dirt circle playing marbles without talking, in a wave of cool morning air laced with honeysuckle. The clicking of the marbles and a June bug's song were as clear in my mind as yesterday's food. Although other things, bigger things, the things we are supposed to remember, were already fading, the cool feel of that slick marble in my hand and the way my bare feet felt in the dust, were sharp in memory. Maybe that's what it all boils down to, I thought, being with a friend on one of God's prettiest mornings.

The preacher's sing-song voice made me want my own words, instead. All-in-all, Burl was okay, I said to myself. He'd made his mistakes all right, but he always had a laugh for you, always had a way of cheering you up. He was a great kidder. And he was tolerant too, real tolerant. Like the way he treated everybody at the factory the same, always looking to see both sides of a thing. I could have gone on more about Burl, remembering how he'd loan me money quick when the need was there, but the singing started up just then and made tears come in my eyes so bad I had to take out my handkerchief. This caused Ellie to give me a quick look and pat me on the arm.

Later on, back at the house, we were sitting at one of the tables set up for the mounds of food left by the neighbors. I never have understood why you have to eat right after a funeral, but sat down with Ellie anyway, everybody just eating away and all talking at the same time. Pretty soon, I got up to get another glass of iced tea—trying not to bother anybody—and stumbled onto something in the kitchen. Now, I know friends and neighbors will hug you to death at a time like this, but this was different. There were Irene and Ken in each other's arms, and he was giving her not a little neighborly peck on the cheek, but a real smackaroo on the mouth. The gold chain around his neck was shining. I never could stand a man who would wear a gold chain. I had seen it early on that day, the name KEN right in the middle. It made me roll my eyes. I don't know what kept me from hitting him, unless it was the way Irene's fingers curled up inside his shirt collar. I backed away quietly and sat back down at the table.

"What's the matter?" Ellie asked me.

"I'll tell you later," I said, then leaned over and whispered, "You'd never believe it."

Just before we left, I looked through the guest book to see who all had been there. Well, I half-looked, I guess, still smarting from what I had witnessed. I put my finger by a name written in large, very bold strokes, which held my attention. The lettering was as clear and sure as any I had ever seen. *Now there's a man who knows what's what,* I said to myself.

Irene, noting my finger pausing over the name, leaned down to read it, her gold necklace moving forward, as well. It was then I noticed the name IRENE, right in the center. Just like Ken's.

"The Cadillac salesman," she told me now. "Wasn't that nice of him to come?"

Sherwood and Dixie

"I've thought and thought about it, Sherwood," she told him, "but I don't see how I can marry you. I just can't change my name, is all. I've had this one too long . . . I'm too *used* to it."

They were no spring chickens, but that was no reason to turn down a man's proposal, Sherwood thought, a little aggravated. "If it's going to be that big a problem," he told her, "we'll just live together."

"Now you know I'm not going to do *that*. Not and have my grandchildren visiting. No, I love you, Sherwood, but I just don't see how we can marry."

They were sitting in her living room. Both lived in a retirement center in Florida and his house was just down the street. It was early spring and a cool breeze was blowing in from the patio, but he could feel the heat on his face. He got up and walked to the patio screen and looked out. "Camelliti is a good name, Dixie."

"Yes, I know, but how could I go from Taylor to Camelliti? It's not like going from Brown to Smith! After all these years it would be . . . like being in disguise or something."

He didn't answer, just remained perfectly still at the patio door.

She said to his back, "Well, there is one way, I guess. We could marry and I could keep my name. Like a lot of women do, these days."

Sherwood turned then and gave her a serious look. "In my book, if you marry a man you should take his name." He came back and sat down across from her so hard he almost knocked off one of the photos on the end table. It happened to be one of her late husband. When Sherwood righted the photo he looked directly at the man in it, and scowled. The man had died ten years ago, but you would think he was still around. Sometimes he felt he would just suffocate with all these family photos of people he mostly didn't know, staring him down. Besides on the two end tables, they covered a good portion of one of the walls in the living room.

"I knew you'd be this way," she said.

"What way?"

"I knew you'd get upset."

"Upset! What have I got to be upset about! Here all this time, I thought we'd be married by summer, and look at us now."

The phone rang then, and Dixie hesitated a few moments, then rose to answer it. He could hear her voice from the other room, talking to her son.

"Well, Sherwood is here right now and we're . . . What? No, I didn't know that." There was a long pause, then, "Look, couldn't we talk about this later on? No, no, I can't keep Susie tomorrow. It really wouldn't be a good time."

Sherwood's shoulders drooped. They had planned for him to stay over tonight, with a nice long, lazy day tomorrow.

"We won't plan a thing," she had told him. "We'll do whatever. comes to mind!"

Her voice hesitated now, was not as self-assured.

"Yes, I . . . suppose so, if that's the only avenue you've got. But couldn't you wait until at least nine?"

Sherwood already had his hand on the front door knob when he heard her saying goodbye to her son, and was down the steps and into his car by the time she realized he was gone.

When he got home, the light was blinking on his machine.

"Sherwood . . ." Dixie's voice implored, "please call me when you get in. We *must* talk."

But he gave in to the reluctance he felt and didn't call, rather put some clothes into the washing machine just to keep the house from being so quiet. He didn't want to put on any music, that would only remind him of her. If they had just met each other years ago, he thought, before all this history built up between them, it might have worked.

He sighed and went to the refrigerator for a beer. But he had only downed half of it, before he picked up the phone.

"Dixie," he said, his voice caving in, "I can't stand it."

"I can't either," she said simply.

So it turned out that Dixie agreed to change her name, and the wedding was set for late summer. Sherwood went along amicably with all the plans, but the part that really excited him was the honeymoon trip they were to take—driving out west in a Winnebago. The fact that he had no experience driving one didn't seem to deter a bit, and Dixie loved the idea of "playing house" in the big camper.

They poured over travel folders and mapped out a trip that would take a whole month.

"A whole month, Dixie!" Sherwood would say, looking up from the folders. "Just you and me." But it was not the thought of all the new places they would see that excited him, but more the thought of traveling in the Winnebago, completely devoid of photos, new to only the two of them, *without anybody's history except that they were making.*

Two weeks before the wedding they had another argument, but this time it was not a name which prompted it.

"What are you going to do with them?" he asked her.

"Do with what?"

"The ashes," he said, gesturing toward the mantle. "Calvin's ashes."

"I hadn't thought of it."

"Well, you better be thinking of it, 'cause they need to be put somewhere. Before this wedding."

"Probably . . . move them somewhere else, I guess."

"That's not what I meant. Ashes are *supposed* to be scattered."

"You know how I feel about that," she said, and looked away.

He well remembered their discussion some time back, about Calvin's ashes. She had not wanted her husband cremated in the first place, she had told him, and said she was just not ready to dispose of the ashes. That conversation was three years ago. And the ashes had remained, where they had always been, in the vase on the mantle.

"If the man wanted to be scattered in the ocean, you should do that for him," Sherwood told her now.

"I know you're right, but I just can't *do* it, Sherwood," she said, then left the room to check on dinner.

He glared at the vase on the mantel and fumed. *I hate that man's ashes,* he whispered to himself. Suddenly Sherwood jumped up, grabbed the vase and shook it hard. But he had not expected a sound to come from it, and when bits of bone hit against the sides of the vase, it so startled him that he almost dropped it. He carefully placed the vase back on the mantel, and sat back down.

"What's the matter?" Dixie said when she returned and noted he was visibly upset.

"Either he goes, or I go," Sherwood said. When she only looked at him with her mouth open, he said "Damned if I'm going to have another's man's ashes in my house."

When he saw her raise her eyes to the ceiling, he started for the door. "It's abnormal not to get buried like everybody else . . . so that when you are gone, you're gone!" he told her. And just before he slammed the screen door he turned back and said, "Everything has a shelf life!"

This time she did not leave a message, and he did not call.

Several weeks went by in which they did not contact each other. Hard weeks, for both.

"What's wrong, mom?" her son asked, concerned about the drawn look on his mother's face, but Dixie would only shake her head, meaning she did not want to talk about it. And the manager of the grocery store where Sherwood shopped, now cringed every time he saw Sherwood enter. He knew it would be only a matter of minutes before Sherwood would charge over to his station, holding up whatever it was that he was dissatisfied with, and complain about the poor condition of the vegetables, or the fact that the meat "looked like hell that week."

Too, the last time Sherwood was in the store he had reached up to take down a box of cereal on the top shelf, and the whole stack underneath fell down on him. The aftermath of *that* spectacle was not one the manager felt he would soon forget.

Out of desperation, Sherwood finally called Dixie.

"Well, I don't see why two people can't even go out to dinner with each other," he told her as soon as she said hello.

She smiled and took a big breath.

"Well I guess I don't, either," she said.

They were cracking crabs at Bill's Crab Shack, when he knew he'd have to bring it up. He hated to do it, they were having such a good time. The breeze coming in the open windows was just right, not to even mention the soft candlelight and the fact that Bill had somebody special singing that night.

But when the words of the singer drifted softly over to their table, all about somebody. "holding onto the past . . . trying to make it last," he looked straight at Dixie and said, "That's what you're doing, Dixie, holding onto the past."

She looked straight back at him and said, "You know something? You never even talk about your former wife. It is as if she never existed!"

"I wish she hadn't. Agnes was the meanest woman God ever created," Sherwood said. And then added quickly, "God rest her soul."

"So, that's it," she said, looking at him very thoughtfully now. "You're clear of the past."

He looked away. "The truth is, Dixie," he started, and then cleared his voice, ". . . you were the first *real* love of my life." Then he brought his eyes back to hers. "There were other women, but none ever moved me like you. None."

He could tell this had got to her. She looked as though she'd like to put her arms around him that very minute. And he was not one to miss an opportunity.

"But, I don't want another man staring me down from the walls or the mantle," he said. "I want us to start brand new."

"All right," she told him, and meant it. She had known in her heart that she would have to take care of Calvin's ashes before a wedding could take place. And she did love Sherwood, there was no doubt about that. "We'll do it Saturday," she said.

Just after sunrise on Saturday morning, they drove out to the beach. It was unusually cool, and both had on long sleeved sweatshirts with their shorts. Sherwood carried the vase as they walked down the beach, looking for just the right spot to sprinkle Calvin's ashes. He thought he had heard somewhere that a person's ashes had to be scattered a mile or two out, to be put in the ocean, but that would have entailed making arrangements for someone to take them out in a boat, and he did not want to waste a minute. He couldn't see what difference it would make anyway, since the ashes would likely be carried out by the current.

"Here," she said, and they finally stopped walking. They could see only one person with a dog, way up ahead, otherwise the beach was deserted.

"Do you want me to do it?" Sherwood asked quietly.

"I wish you would," she said.

It was a solemn moment. They walked out a ways into the water and Sherwood began to ready the vase. "Wait . . ." she said. "We have to say something."

Oh boy, he was thinking. He knew there had been a memorial service years ago, so he had not expected this. But she had already started up.

"Calvin, she said, looking partly at the vase and partly at the sky beyond, . . . we are doing it, honey . . . just what you wanted."

It galled Sherwood to hear her say the word *honey*, but he only listened. "I'm . . . we're getting married soon, this man and I."

Sherwood thought he'd better say something then, and threw out, "I'll be good to her, Calvin."

She smiled, though kept her eyes on the vase now. Suddenly her face turned very serious. "Oh, I *do* hope you are okay . . . I really do. I do hope that wherever you are, you are happy." Her eyes became misty then, and she nodded to Sherwood and he took the top off the vase and raised it high—then turned it upside down. Just before the wind took the ashes Dixie turned away, and gazed far up to the sky.

Sherwood had not calculated on the direction of the wind, and was appalled when some of the contents blew back on his shorts. Though the wind was carrying most away, he tried desperately to brush the remainder off, but his hands were too full with the vase.

"Damn, *Damn*" he muttered under his breath. Luckily, Dixie was still gazing up to the sky with her back to him, and the sound of the ocean covered his words.

When they were walking back to the car, Sherwood kept brushing his shorts, over and over again. But Dixie, lost in her own thoughts, never noticed. Not even when Sherwood—about to put the key into the ignition—looked down to see the imprint of something in his shorts pocket and thinking it possibly a sliver of bone, yelled. When he jumped out of the car and emptied the pockets, a shell he had forgotten he picked up, fell out on the ground.

"What on earth was it?" Dixie said, when he got back into the car. "A bee?"

When Sherwood got home he threw the shorts into a trash bin, and took a shower for almost forty-five minutes.

"Damn it," he kept yelling, over and over again.

When things finally settled, a kind of peace came to both of them, now that the ashes were gone. They got back to pouring over the plans for the wedding, and their trip. The wedding was to be at her house, with just family and a few friends. Sherwood's only living relative, a brother, was coming down from Poughkeepsie.

The day of the wedding, Sherwood had a big smile on his face as he walked down to Dixie's house. But it was not the nuptials he had on his mind. He was thinking of the Winnebago, waiting back there in his driveway—waiting pristine, with no photos, no ashes, no past. Just the future. Waiting for Mr. and Mrs. Camelliti to take off.

One month later, when they returned from the trip out West, Sherwood turned off the ignition and they sat for a moment, just looking at the house. Dixie put her hand over his and said, "Well, we are home." She was smiling. He put his other hand over hers and squeezed.

But as he walked down the hallway with their suitcases, he was aware of all the photographs on the periphery as he passed the living room. He sighed. They are, indeed, home.

Dixie was flipping through the mail and stopped when she saw a packet from her son. She opened the end and pulled out pictures he had made at the wedding.

"Oh, Sherwood," she called out, "come and see."

He sat the last of the bags down and looked over her shoulder.

"They are from Barry. He made them at the wedding. Sit with me." He sat beside her, and they began to look at the photos.

"Ha! Those tin cans tied to the Winnabego," Sherwood said.

"What a racket we made getting out of town!" She showed him another photo. "See . . . everybody waving at us from the curb. I'll have them all blown up and put into frames!"

Sherwood turned toward the wall of photos.

"*Our* pictures," he said softly, as if to himself.

"Look at this one, Sherwood. Isn't it *dear?* You holding little Samuel, just before we left."

Sherwood looked at the photo very carefully.

"The youngest grandchild. The baby. They never thought they'd have one this late."

"I remember he held my finger so tight. . . ."

"You are the only grandfather he knows. At least on this side of the family.

"I am, aren't I? I *really* am," he said, awed, as if just discovering it himself.

"Yes. He'll bond with you," she told him.

"Blow this one up big, Dixie," he said excited now. He went to the wall and pointed to the very center of all the photos. "And put it here. Right here."

Dixie came and stood next to him. She put her arm around his waist as they envisioned the photo in just that very spot.

"I'll call him Sammy.

"I think they want to stick to Samuel.

"That's no name for a kid.

"Well, that's what they decided on.

43

Sherwood gave it some thought.

"Well, over here, he can relax. He can be Sammy.

"I'll put this one right next to it," she said, showing Sherwood another photo. "The one of us . . . Mr. and Mrs Camelliti."

"Ahhhh, Dixie. You make my heart grow."

Dixie put her head on his shoulder as they stood looking at the wall, envisioning the pictures.

"We'll put up the ones of the Winnebago, too. How you loved playing house in that Winnebago, Dixie."

"And you finally got the hang of it, didn't you?"

"I knew I would. I'm a good driver," he said, somewhat indignant.

Dixie turned and gave him a look.

"Well I am! What did it take me . . . two, three days, to master that buggy?"

"More like two to three weeks, I think."

"Now, you know that's not the truth, Dixie."

"Why in the world would I make it up?"

"Well somebody is not telling the truth here, and it's not me!"

"Oh, Sherwood!"

Myrtice

Myrtice Holt had a great longing. All of her life she had wanted to own property, had wanted to hold a deed in her hand with her name on it. But circumstances always stood in the way. Hard circumstances. Now she was getting close to the latter phase of her life, and still this dream remained unfulfilled. She thought she had given up on it. But one day, while placing flowers on a friend's grave, a little flag making a flapping sound caught her attention and caused her to look out over the cemetery. The flag was on a grave, just across the tiny road. Myrtice saw that the area was shaded by a beautiful old oak tree, and seemed quite peaceful. It was situated on the far edge of the hill, and was designated as "The Garden of Meditation."

Later, as she drove out, she noticed a sign just before the big double gate: Attention Property Owners. Come by the office to update your records.

She could not get that sign, and the words "Property Owners," out of her mind. The next day she drove all the way back to Oakdale Cemetery and walked straight into the office. "I'm interested in a plot," she said, ". . . for myself." The manager, Mr. Hunnicut, was only too happy to show her what was available. He got out his book, but she was already pointing beyond the window. "See that big oak tree," she said, "What do you have over there?"

"Well, let's just take a look," he told her, opening the record book. "We fill up the areas near the trees first, so you might have to

45

settle for something else." He ran his hand down a list, his finger stopping at Number 143. "Looks like you are in luck, but I'm going to check the computer, too, just to be sure." The computer was already on, and all the man had to do was click a couple of keys and there it was. She looked over his shoulder. Number 143 Meditation Lane, almost called out to her. Myrtice noted the line was blank.

"I'd like to see that one," she said, before he could even suggest.

The plot was on the same hill, not far from the little flapping flag, and well under the shade of the big tree. She liked it immediately.

"The adjoining area is also available for another family member, should you want it."

"There is just me," she said, looking out over the hill. She could see the chapel down below. "Do they ever have services there?"

He followed her gaze. "Yes, though not often," he told her. "And sometimes," he said, "an occasional wedding."

"A wedding. Here?"

"Yes. We get the request once every year or so, which we usually grant but make them keep it small."

"Seems a strange place for a wedding."

"It appears quite apt to me," he said smiling, ". . . given today's statistics."

It wasn't long before the certificate Mr. Hunnicut had handed her that day got dog-eared from opening and closing so many times. She loved to see her name on the line that declared her as "Owner of the Property." It elicited a big smile every time she looked at it. Finally, she made herself file the paper away in her lock-box.

The "property" stayed in her mind like a secondary thing, under all other activities. So that on her way home from shopping it seemed only natural to turn right instead of left, and take the road to the cemetery.

When she got out of the car and stood under the tree in the area of her plot, she experienced a feeling of such elation it almost took her breath. She breathed the feeling in deep, raising her arms slightly at her sides. She had thought it would fade—but here it was, filling her up all over again. She had done it at last! Finally had her own land. She envisioned her name, Myrtice P. Holt, carved on the future stone, much as a door knocker might denote *Jones* or *Smith*. Only her name would stay there forever, she told herself, not like a house that could be sold to others. This plot would never belong to anyone but her. Once this thought took hold, it not only lessened past regret over not owning property, but surpassed. A house, after all, could be sold many times over.

Myrtice began to go by the cemetery every other day. Once a woman walked up to her and said, "I don't want to disturb you, but I've noticed you come here often and . . . I just want to say I'm so sorry for your loss."

"No, no. I'm not mourning," Myrtice told her. "It's just . . . it's my place, you see."

"Your place?"

"Yes. This is my plot."

"Oh."

"My home, you might say." And then, noting the woman's eyes widening, added, "I won't be able to enjoy it, later. And it is so nice here . . . this lovely old tree, the wonderful shade, the sweet breezes."

The woman just nodded slowly and walked away. Looking after her, Myrtice whispered *My first visitor,* as if the first visiting neighbor had popped in.

Just then, someone throwing something at a grave and talking loud, caught Myrtice's attention, and she peeked around the oak tree, and listened.

"You jerk!" the woman said, "Did you think I'd never see your credit card bills? But then, you didn't anticipate dying, did you? Betrayed on the Interstate by your precious Mercedes."

She threw more stones. "Lingerie, flowers . . . dinners at restaurants you never *once* took me to!" She threw another stone, this one bigger than before, hitting the new tombstone with a loud clunk.

"And that fur jacket . . . that *mink* jacket . . ." She lowered her voice then, "If you think I'm lying here, next to you when I die, you can rot in hell, first!"

At that Myrtice had to stifle a giggle.

Then the woman stormed over to her car and took off in a cloud of dust, well exceeding the cemetery speed limit.

It seemed a never-ending parade of happenings. Myrtice was fascinated with the people who came and all the things going on in the cemetery, even the workers who appeared every day.

When she noted grave diggers working nearby, she walked over to watch.

"Hello," she said. There were two men and one tipped his sun hat. The other continued with his shoveling.

"I've often wondered what it must be like. To be a grave digger, I mean," Myrtice said. Neither of the men responded.

"Well, I guess it is like any other job, really. But still. . . ."

"No difference, lady. You got a job, you do it," one of the men told her, then went back to work as if dismissing it. The other said, "It's all done mostly by machine now. We just finish up."

"I guess what I mean is . . . this particular job must be a little different?"

Both of the men quietly continued shoveling dirt into the hole.

"It's not like you are selling insurance or anything."

One turned then, and looked directly at her.

"I've had other occupations," he said irritably, then took another shovelful of dirt and tossed it into the deep hole.

"Oh, I didn't mean. . . ."

"It's a job, like I told you. Just a job," the man said. He was panting hard.

"Well, I guess you must find interesting items," she said. "Occasionally."

Both men stopped now and looked at her.

"I've heard some people will throw in something, on top of the casket . . . a locket, some memento . . . before it's covered over with dirt."

They stared at her intently. Their faces were serious.

"I mean, that's what I've heard."

"We don't keep stuff lady."

"Oh, no, I didn't mean . . . I'm sure you don't. But, do you cover it up? Or give it to the cemetery manager?

"Cover it up," one answered, picking up his shovel again.

"Would you go down there?" the other said, pointing to the dark hole.

Myrtice leaned over the rim and looked. "Nooooooo," she said. It was then she noticed Mr. Hunnicut's car.

"Mrs. Holt," he called out from his window, ". . . may I see you a moment?"

Myrtice walked over to the car.

"It's not seemly to carry on conversations with the grave diggers," he told her.

"I was just curious."

"Yes, well, some of them can be very unscrupulous people." He started up the car. "Besides that, they are supposed to be working!"

There was a small caretaker's house on the grounds, though Myrtice never saw him, except when he was riding on his mower. Once, she hurried over to introduce herself when she spotted him emptying a trash container, but when she got there he was gone—as if only an aberration. Another time she tried to catch him as he was putting materials in his little truck. But then she saw him quickly throw the last item into the back, and jump in. She felt sure he had seen her wave.

Often when Myrtice came, she cleared and weeded the plot. Afterward she felt as though she had given a house a good cleaning. Once she planted some flowers, though she knew it was against the rules. It gave her a good feeling to know the seeds were there—her seeds, in her soil. She wouldn't worry about the rules until the flowers came up, in early summer. And then they would be so beautiful, she thought, surely the cemetery manager would let her keep them.

From her vantage point on the hill, she watched many graveside funerals, saw the little groups huddled under the canopies, saw the long limousines waiting at the curbs. People grieving caused her own compassion to grow. Remembering her own hard griefs, she was sometimes overwhelmed with wanting to console.

One morning while driving into the cemetery, Myrtice noticed a woman bent almost double in the children's section, so wrought with grief it appeared she could not get her breath. Myrtice stopped the car and got out quietly, then walked over and put her arm around the woman's shoulder and patted her back, saying,

"I know. I know." She turned immediately to Myrtice and began to sob uncontrollably. After what seemed a long time, the sobbing subsided, and Myrtice left. The woman later told Mr. Hunnicut that a wonderful lady had helped her.

"An angel, really," and pointed toward the oak tree on the hill, where Myrtice was standing.

Another time, Myrtice approached a young man who was openly grieving.

"Your mother?" she asked. He didn't even look up, only shook his head no.

"Your wife, then? "Yes, *yes*," he said, still looking down.

"Don't worry, you'll see her again," she told him. And there was such certainty in her voice, he looked up. When she saw his eyes, they broke her heart.

"It's true," she told him, ". . . this is just a passage. That's all." When he did not answer, but cast his mournful eyes back toward the grave, Myrtice said, "Love has staying power" and walked away. The words hung in the air, turning his head.

Her conviction was more instinctive than religious. She knew—beyond any doubt—that life, in some fashion, went on after death. It was the same instinct that woke her at three a.m. with a feeling of foreboding that told her the son she had loved so dearly for eight years, might not make it to his ninth. And it was this same deep seated instinct that told her the boy's father—an obsessed, near penniless artist—would leave her one cold winter day, and never come back. It was because of him she had no house.

"We need to be free," he'd say, "Can't you see that!"

But she had never seen their long succession of apartments as freedom, nor their moving from city to city. Then after he left her, a great sadness muffled the desire for property—at least for a while. Later, she simply couldn't figure out how to go about it alone. Not on a waitress' salary, and that had been the only job she could get, with all their moving around. Too late now, anyway, she finally told herself.

But here, at last, she had a bit of property, and it gave her a true sense of peace. In late spring she brought a lawn chair, and often read or knitted in the shade. Currently, she was reading poetry. The quiet surroundings seemed to deepen the poems, causing her to look up from time to time and consider their meanings, or to meditate on her own life. She wondered why more people had not discovered the calming quiet of cemeteries. She felt she could not have owned land anywhere in the entire city that would be more peaceful.

Early one morning she drove through the big cemetery gates and found herself the only one around—no visitors, no grave diggers about, and even the caretaker's curtains were still closed. It was very quiet, except for the birds and the faint sound of muffled traffic beyond the rim of the cemetery. She appeared utterly alone. Looking far out, over the rows and rows of tombstones, she wondered why some people thought of cemeteries as fearful places. It's not the ones in here that I fear, she thought, it's the ones out there . . . where I have to lock my doors.

Right after she started bringing the lawn chair, Mr. Hunnicut came and asked if she was all right. "Oh, I'm just fine," she told him, "Just enjoying this wonderful breeze!"

He looked at her very carefully, then asked in a cautious voice, "You're satisfied with the plot, then?"

"Oh, yes! It's a perfect place here, under the tree. And the hill affords such a lovely view."

"You . . . you come often, don't you?"

"Yes. It gives me a great sense of peace."

When he didn't say anymore, she added, "It's all right, isn't it?"

"Well it's your plot," he said. "Not many people do it, is all." Then added, "Unless visiting someone actually buried."

"Well . . . it's much more pleasant this way."

"I expect so," he said, walking on, then turned back and added, "You know we do have benches."

"Yes, but they are stone and very hard, and much too far away."

He just nodded and walked on, not wanting to get into it.

Often, seeing her lawn chair for the first time, people would slow up as they drove by, and stare at the woman reading, saying things like, "Poor thing—her husband's grave, no doubt." Or simply, "tsk, tsk, tsk," and shake their heads. Mr. Hunnicut waited for someone to complain, but no one ever did.

Myrtice started bringing her lunch—usually a sandwich and a bottle of fruit juice—which she kept in a container in the car until she was sure Mr. Hunnicut was not around. She liked to eat her lunch in the spring sun, and had to move the lawn chair slightly out of her area of shade to do it. Sometimes, if it was an especially warm day she would rub on a little sun lotion, holding her arms high as she did so, and being especially mindful of putting a dollop on her nose.

It was around this time that she found herself writing 143 Meditation Lane, as a return address, on the corner of an envelope. It had felt so natural, it took a moment for her to realize the mistake. Then she remembered she had done the same on another envelope, but that one had already been mailed. Oh, well, she thought, what difference does it make after all?

A week or so later Mr. Hunnicut brought a letter over to her as she sat in her chair. "Is this yours?" he asked.

When Myrtice saw the letter with the stamped words, "Address Unknown. Return to Sender," she realized the letter she had mailed with the cemetery address penned in the upper left corner, had been returned. She blushed.

"I . . . must have absentmindedly written this address, instead of my home address."

Mr. Hunnicut shook his head and sighed. "Be sure not to do it again," he told her. "Our staff is overloaded, as it is."

Myrtice began to feel she knew the people who came to visit the surrounding graves.

"You just missed your daughter," she called out cheerfully to one. "She was here, earlier."

Soon various people stopped by to say hello to Myrtice, and Mr. Hunnicut took note with a little worried frown.

She continued to console, wherever she noted the need. There was something in her that connected, some special openness, and people responded. Even, the irate stone thrower, who had come back to her husband's grave, talking about something she was going to do to spite him—something regarding the money he left—whacking the stone at the end of her loud words, with her pocketbook. Myrtice, came from behind the tree this time, and said,

"No. No, you don't want to do that." When the woman wheeled around and stared at her, Myrtice said,

"Wait a year to make any big decisions . . . that's what they all say." The woman, frowning, kept staring. "I'm sorry," Myrtice told her, ". . . but I couldn't help overhearing."

The woman's face softened, then.

"A year? A whole year?" she asked Myrtice.

Every day, on her way out, Myrtice drove by three huge vaults and pondered the same question: Why would anyone want something like that? Once she asked Mr. Hunnicut.

"Vanity . . . or pomp, maybe fear," he answered.

"Fear?" she said. "What do you mean?

"Fear of worms, maggots, you name it," he told her. "But, I'd say mostly it is vanity."

Occasionally she attended a graveside service, standing just behind the little group and listening, generally clucking over the ministers eulogy. For the most part, they puffed it up a bit too much to suit her. Nobody's that good, she'd whisper to herself.

Sometimes, as she sat reading or knitting, the sun moved over the shadows of the tombstones and highlighted a name. Morris, Taplinger, Cunningham; she was beginning to feel they were all acquaintances. She liked to imagine what their lives might have been.

One day, a big collie lying across a new grave caught her attention, and she went to pet and talk softly to the dog. Shortly, someone came with a leash.

"His owner's grave," the man said. "We don't know how he knew to come here but he jumps the fence almost every day." The man put the leash on the dog, and tugged gently. "Strange isn't it?" he said to Myrtice, "How some animals know these things?"

"Yes," she answered. "A real mystery."

The man tugged again. "Come on, Brandy," he said, and the dog got up and followed him to the car.

Once she saw two people stealing flowers from a grave site where a funeral had recently been held, and quickly let Mr. Hunnicut know. He thanked her and immediately called the police, though by the time they got there the thieves were gone.

After that, Mr. Hunnicut decided not to say anything about her chair. Even stopped by from time to time, to ask if she had noticed anything else out of the ordinary.

"Be sure to let me know if you see anything suspicious again. And get the license number, if you can." It was then she noted the careful trim of his grey beard. Not like the wild, unruly one her husband had.

In May, when the flowers began to come up, Myrtice was overjoyed. She picked some and took them to graves she knew were never visited. Placing them made her wonder who would come and place flowers on her own grave, having no children now, and no living relatives, to speak of. One thing she knew for sure, she never wanted any plastic flowers! No flowers would be better than plastic.

Mr. Hunnicut phoned her shortly after he discovered the flowers. She was in her tiny apartment kitchen, making a meatloaf, when the phone rang.

"We can't have people planting things here," he told her. "We have a rule, it's listed in your papers," he said. "I let you do everything else. But this, we cannot do."

"Why? People bring flowers all the time."

"That's different," he told her.

She was quiet a moment, then said,

"Do you like meatloaf sandwiches?"

When he didn't answer, she said,

"I could bring you one tomorrow, for your lunch."

"The flowers really have to go," he said.

She gave it one more try—"I'll have no one to bring flowers . . . when I'm gone."

There was a lengthy pause. She could hear him breathing, and a long sigh.

"I'm sorry, but you must come and take them home, or the gardener will mow over them."

"Oh, no!" she said. "Not mow them."

Early the next morning she hurried out to the cemetery. Mr. Hunnicut was checking the work of some grave diggers nearby, when he saw her car slow down at the old oak, and watched her get out. At first she just looked at the flowers, then stooped and stroked them tenderly. When she tried to pull one up by the root, she stopped, then took a hankie to her eyes.

Mr. Hunnicut's body slumped. He put his hands to his forehead and rubbed it over and over again, in an exasperated manner. Then, reluctantly, he walked over and told her she could keep the flowers one more week.

"But just one," he told her seriously.

"Oh, bless you!" she said, wiping her eyes.

She came every day, then. And lavished all her attention on the flowers—pruning, petting, and talking to them. When the week was up, she brought her scissors and cut them all, taking them again to various graves, saving only one for herself. When she departed that day, driving by all the graves graced with her flowers made her happy. Real flowers, not plastic.

Near the end of summer, Myrtice's hearing had grown so acute from sitting quietly in the cemetery, that a slight rustle of wind in the top of a tree would cause her to look up, or a squirrel suddenly scampering would cause her to jump. Her olfactory senses became heightened as well, inducing her to close her eyes and breathe deeply over the scent of freshly cut grass, or recently placed roses, though some distance away.

In the fall Myrtice stopped taking her power walks in a local park, and took them in the cemetery instead, wearing her running shoes and sport outfits. She would start out fast, getting into the rapid pace she was used to, arms swinging high at her sides, her long legs taking her around the whole area in record time. It was really more a run, than a walk.

But a few days later, Mr. Hunnicut noticed her streak by his window, and ran right after her. He had to speed by the Garden of Wisdom, and then the Garden of the Chalice, before he could catch up, breathlessly taking her arm.

"We can't do this!" he said, trying to breathe slower. "It's not seemly. This is a cemetery! Not a marathon."

She stared at his face. She didn't know if the green in his eyes was so vivid because the cloudy day had accentuated colors, but they were the most striking she'd ever seen.

"Well?" he said when she didn't answer.

She smiled at him then. "All right," she said, "I'll try to walk slower."

Soon, all the quiet Myrtice had reveled in was replaced by the hammering of construction workers who were erecting a large circular building, to replace the old cemetery office. After trying to read with great effort, and having her walks disturbed by constant noise, Myrtice finally marched into Mr. Hunnicut's office, took him to the window and pointed to the rows of tombstones.

"All those people who bought lots in what they thought would be a quiet, peaceful cemetery, can't complain. So I am going to be their spokesperson," she told him.

"Mrs. Holt, settle down. What are you talking about?"

"All this construction going on. The noise is excruciating! You can't even hear the carillon anymore. And I'm sure that's another reason people bought plots here . . . that soothing peaceful sound of the carillon."

"It will all be over in another month," he said, returning to his desk.

"Another whole month!"

"It's a large building. It can't be finished overnight."

"It looks like some big, ugly mausoleum, anyway. It's just awful! And I'll tell you something else," she said, leaning over his desk, her voice geared to a confidential tone, "The whole thing is just not seemly." Then she turned and walked out of the office, but not before she had seen him out of the corner of her eye strike his desk hard with a paper, as if doing battle with a fly.

It was the distraction of the construction which kept Mr. Hunnicut and others from noticing that the flower thieves had returned. Too, there was a rash of funerals, and it was not unusual for five, even six services a day to be held, with huge baskets and sprays of beautiful flowers left behind at the grave sites.

Myrtice, by now, had become adjusted to the noise of the construction. At first, she had tried to stay home in her apartment, but found she missed the cemetery too much. The day of her return she discovered the thieves.

The two men were parked in a big van, not far from Myrtice's plot. They had seen her bring her chair over to the area (which raised their eyebrows), and were now restlessly waiting for her to finish her lunch (which had raised their eyebrows even more). She was eating very slowly, as if thinking about something. The men had spotted only one other person in the immediate area—someone who had brought red roses to a nearby grave. They had not had to wait as long for him.

Myrtice had seen the roses, too—big, beautiful red roses in a large, heart-shaped spray, and recognized the young man who had lost his wife. She saw him kneel quietly, moving his mouth as if talking, and knew not to disturb him. When she heard his car leave, she got out her sun lotion and settled back in the chair, stretching her arms out as usual as she applied the lotion. Afterward, she adjusted the lawn chair so that she could lie back flat, and then closed her eyes.

"A nut case. A friggin' nut case!" one of the men said.

The other man sat frowning and drumming his fingers on the dash. Finally, he suggested they go ahead anyway. "She wouldn't know what we were doing. Look at her . . . she's in her own world. Probably dreaming she is in the Caribbean, right now."

"I don't know . . . she could screw it up. Let's go on. We've got enough flowers."

"No. This site has the biggest baskets," his partner answered. Then he gave Myrtice a long look. "You know what to do if there's trouble."

"Yeah," the man answered, but his voice was uneasy.

The way they generally worked was for one to go and stand at a tombstone near a site where fresh flowers were left from one of the funerals. He would stand there, hat dutifully over his heart, shoulders folded in, and with a studied look of deep sorrow keep watch as the other quickly put flowers into the back of the van. But unbeknown to the men, Myrtice had heard every word—not so much because the car windows were open, but because her hearing had grown so acute these last months in the cemetery. Too, the construction hammering had stopped momentarily. She waited—still as a corpse—for them to begin.

First, she calculated the path from her heightened sense of smell. Though her eyes were completely closed, she sensed the flowers being moved quickly from various areas in the cemetery back to the van.

She slowly opened one eye. She could see one of the men—in his posture of grief—standing lookout at a grave site, while the other scurried past the tree, his arms full of flower baskets. Myrtice concentrated on any description she could get of the two men. The license number was going to be harder; she would have to turn to see it and she did not want to move. Then something happened to trigger her courage. She had to close her eyes each time she heard the soft shuffle of shoes coming down the path, but now her sharpened listening told her the path had changed, and all of a sudden she could distinctly smell the red roses. Myrtice was incensed. Not the roses.

The heart shaped roses! Off in the distance she saw Brandy, lying as usual on his master's grave. She sat up quickly and called to him, "Get him Brandy!" she yelled, and the dog started after the man as Myrtice ran toward the cemetery office. But then she remembered the license number, and turned back. Brandy had "treed" the first man—legs tucked under on a tall monument—and now loped after the other, barking loudly. The man jumped into the van and started the engine. When the car began to move, Brandy ran right along the side, with Myrtice—whose power walks had seemed to prepare her just for this feat—running right behind, yelling the license number over and over again to herself: "JEF2942 . . . JEF2942." Long faced people who were just coming out from one of the canopies, stood by the edge of the little road with their mouths open, watching a woman try to outrun a car.

Mr. Hunnicut, noting all the commotion from his window, called 911 and got his jacket.

The whole thing was on the front page of the paper the next morning, including Myrtice's picture with the caption: Woman Helps Expose Florist Ring. It turned out the men were part of a ring of flower thieves, who worked out of a central florist shop in the city where stolen flowers were immediately resold. Some people recognized her photo in the paper.

"That's the cemetery lady!" they said, putting their fingers on the picture of a smiling Myrtice. Soon crowds of people came for her autograph.

"But I'm not anybody," she told them.

"Oh, but you are!" they said.

Mr. Hunnicut, who had at first admired her bravery, was now gravely concerned. But soon it all settled down, Myrtice had her fifteen minutes of fame, and things got back to normal in the cemetery. Mr. Hunnicut could breathe again.

When the weather got colder, Myrtice often took her walk in a long, red coat. She was a tall woman, tall and stately, and her long red coat stood out among the grey tombstones. The spot of red would draw Mr. Hunnicut's eye to the window. He had often thought her striking, standing on the hill like a character out of a book, but now noted something regal about the way she walked, with her head high, shoulders back. Once he said softly outloud,

"An attractive woman, even so."

In the heart of the winter, when all the leaves had blown from the oak tree and the wind cut right through her heavy coat, Myrtice stayed in the car—parked just in front of her property— reading, or listening to classical music on the radio. The bare arms of the tree hovered over the roof of the car.

She began to relive her life. It unfolded there, under the old tree, showing her scenes from the past, scenes that had taken their toll—the cold hospital room where she stared at the wall the day her son died from an auto accident. She remembered the sliver of light that came and went when the nurse cracked the door and then closed it softly, not having the heart to bother her. She saw herself walking, that day—walking and walking, all over the city, trying not to go home, as if she could only keep on walking she might keep alive the possibility that it wasn't true. Then she saw herself another time, a cruel winter morning, waking up slowly, trying not to turn her head too soon on the pillow, trying not to see the empty space she somehow already knew was there beside her.

So many harsh happenings, she thought, looking now toward the children's section of the cemetery. She wished her son was buried here, instead of in that distant city. That was one time she had begged her husband to stay, though in the end they had left that small grave, and moved on. She had agreed to that at first, thinking it would be too painful to visit his grave, anyway. But now she wished otherwise.

The car was becoming quite cold, though lost in reverie, she was not aware. She began to think of things she wished she could have done differently. Once she broke out into tears, and it was as if she were mourning herself, there in that cemetery, before the fact. Mourning the person she could have been. So late, she thought.

Mr. Hunnicut, having seen her car earlier and knowing how cold she must be by now, sighed and put down his pen, his eyes drawn to the window. It appeared to him that she might be crying and he sighed again, louder this time, and got up and went for his coat. Thank God he was retiring soon, he thought.

"Mrs. Holt," he said, tapping on her car window. "Is everything okay?"

She blew her nose and shook her head no.

He opened the car door. "May I?" he asked.

She shook her head yes, and patted the seat once.

After settling himself inside the car, he simply waited. In a moment she said,

"Life is hard, isn't it?" and blew her nose again.

"Seems that way, sometimes," he said.

"Do you ever regret things, Mr. Hunnicut?"

"Everybody regrets some things," he told her.

"No. I mean, do you ever wish you could live some part of your life over?" she asked, a great heaviness in her voice.

He could have avoided all this if he'd only stayed in the office, he thought. But the look on her sad face seemed so expectant of an honest answer that he felt he would at least try. He looked away toward the old oak, and dug deep.

"I wish I had married," he said, finally.

"You never got married?" Her voice was incredulous.

"No . . . I loved someone, but waited too long to tell her."

"What happened?"

"She married somebody else."

"I'm sorry."

"Long time ago," he said. "I never think of it now."

"But it came to mind . . . first," she told him.

He turned back to her, then. "Yes, yes it did, didn't it."

She gazed thoughtfully out the window a moment.

"I wish I'd done more," she said. "Not wasted a precious minute." Then she looked directly at him. "Do you?"

Her eyes were lovely, he thought. Such feeling in them. Such honest feeling.

"Of course," he told her. And then, "I wish I'd been a reporter, that's what I always wanted to do."

"You could still write, couldn't you? When you retire?" And before he could answer, she said, "And what a world of things to write about, having been a cemetery manager!"

He had not thought of that. Never even considered it, and yet, he could see himself doing this very thing, now. And Lord knows, this job had afforded him stories, he thought.

"Yes," he said, "I guess I could." He had never known a woman so easy to talk to.

"And you," he said softly, "What do you wish you had done?"

At that moment, a little red cardinal—perched on a tombstone just a few yards away— began to sing out in clear, high tones. The sound, so close, seemed to pierce right through Myrtice.

"I wish I had had more love in my life," she said.

Her words hung in the air; he had no answer for them.

The bells of the carillon were ringing off in the distance, and the sound seemed muffled in the closed car. A light snow was just beginning to fall all around them, now dotting the windshield.

"I've heard so many people here say they wish they had done things differently, when a loved one dies," he told her. "Regret is a word I hear a lot on this job. And yet, they almost all realize, sooner or later, that they did the best they could." He looked out the window at the cardinal; the bird was quiet now, as if listening to them. "Everyone has some regret, it seems," he said.

"I wish I had gone to college," she blurted out. "I think about that a lot. I married very young."

"You can certainly do that now, with all the on-line college classes on computer."

"I never thought of that."

"Sure," he told her. "If you really want it, it's possible."

She sat up a little straighter in the seat and tried to see herself doing this. "I don't even know how to use a computer," she said.

"You'd catch on quickly . . . you have a good mind."

"Oh, I don't know."

"Just take a few classes and see."

"It's not that I want a career this late," she told him. "I just want to learn."

"Well then, just do it!"

She saw herself actually sitting at a computer now. Maybe it is possible, she thought. Maybe it really is.

He rubbed his gloves together. "You know, I've got hot cocoa in my office. Would you like to go there and get warm?"

"That would be nice."

To anyone driving by, the two people sitting in front of the manager's window in the new building, blowing on steaming cups of hot cocoa and smiling at each other, seemed an amicable couple, or at the very least, old friends. He had been telling her some "funny" things that had happened to him as cemetery manager, and she was laughing. No one had ever laughed at his stories before.

Myrtice put her cup down and looked out of the big office window at the snow, now beginning to stick on the tombstones.

"When I was a child and it snowed, I used to hold my arms out and twirl around with my face up to the sky, catching snowflakes on my tongue," she told him. "I feel like that now . . . like I'd like to go and twirl around the tombstones, and catch snowflakes on my tongue."

He put his hand on one of hers as if to stay her. "But you won't, really. Will you?"

She smiled and looked directly into his green eyes. They were *such* different people, she thought, but still . . . "No," she said, "Not right now."

His hand relaxed on hers, though he left it a moment or two. She was the most vexing, aggravating, exasperating woman he had ever met in his life—yet the most compelling. Suddenly he knew that if she had gone and done what she had just described, he would have only smiled.

"Are you retiring soon?" she asked him. She had heard talk of it, in the office.

"In a few months," he told her.

"Maybe . . . you'd like to come by for coffee sometime," she said. "After you retire, I mean."

"Which address?" he asked in a teasing voice.

"Oh, I won't be coming back to the cemetery, now. Too cold. And anyway, I think I'll try your suggestion." When he gave her a quizzical look, she said, "The computer classes."

"Good idea!" he said. And in a moment he added, "You know, we wouldn't have to wait until I retire to have that coffee, sometime."

"No, I guess not," she said to him. Then, "What is your first name?

"Henry."

"Henry Hunnicut," she said, trying out the words. "I'm Myrtice."

He laughed. "I know." And still chuckling, he excused himself to prepare for closing up.

"I'll only be a minute," he said. Then I'll walk you out."

Myrtice looked out of the window again. Purple streaks in the sky were just fading into the early winter dusk. Here and there, all was lit by snow, the shiny whiteness like sparkling points of light. She glanced up at the old tree on the hill, its bare branches now covered over with snow, standing like a beacon. Soon, in the spring, it will be sprouting again, she thought. New beginnings. This past year, she had seen the tree in all its glory— especially in the fall—but somehow, to her, this pared down bareness had the real substance.

Verna

Verna sat tight-lipped, pretending to read the paper, still seething over her sister's comment. She had never married, but it was more from demeanor, than choice; she was bitter and it showed. *I want to fight!* those eyes seemed to say.

"Born bitter," her mother had often remarked.

After their mother died, Verna moved in with her father "to take care of him," she declared to all, although it seemed as though he were the caretaker. Now she turned the pages of the newspaper hard, popping them out as her sister, Jane, tried again to explain.

"At least take your face out of the paper," Jane told her.

Verna slid the paper down from her eyes and scowled.

"As usual, you take offense at anything that is said to you. What I *meant* was that your hair looked different, that's all. Not bad, just different. I assume you've had it cut?"

"Any idiot can see that," Verna said and went back to the paper.

"Could we just move on to another subject?" Jane asked in a tired voice.

"Jane. I was *trying* to read." She reached over and snapped on the table light and buried her face even further in the paper.

The room was always shadowy, not just because of the eaves but more from Verna's insistence on keeping the drapes partially closed all the time. She and her father had argued about this, until he finally gave up and got used to the dim room.

"You wouldn't have to turn on that light if you'd open these drapes more. Let in some natural light, for a change."

Verna just kept her head down.

"Now hear me out, Verna. Daddy's birthday is Saturday and we need to plan something."

"Why?" Verna said in a disinterested voice from behind the paper.

"Because it's his *birthday*, that's why!" Jane said, drumming her fingers impatiently. "Anyway, I think maybe fixing his favorite dinner and one of us making a cake should do it."

"I'm not making the man a cake, Jane. I can tell you that, right now."

"Oh, *why* did I even mention it."

Verna looked at her now. "Yes, why? Why on earth couldn't you just make the silly cake and bring it over here? But no, you have to go on and on about it."

"How am I to know that you and Daddy wouldn't plan something different?" Jane said, her voice rising. "Unless I ask!"

"Do we ever plan anything different?"

Jane sighed. "Well, I would certainly have thought you'd appreciate somebody helping you with a birthday dinner."

"I don't plan on even acknowledging it."

"What is it this time, Verna? What could it *possibly* be now."

"The man has not apologized to me, and until he does, I certainly do not intend to celebrate his birthday."

"Can't you ever get off Daddy!"

"You should have heard him. Asked me if I'd put on weight, said maybe I should diet. Then had the *nerve* to tell me the buttons looked strained on my skirt!"

"Oh, he didn't mean anything by that. He's just talking."

"And there's something else. "

"What?"

"I'm not sure I'm in the mood to divulge it."

"That's it," Jane said, getting up and starting toward the door.

Verna put the paper on the end table, and then blurted it out.

"He is seeing Thelma Nobles."

"What?"

"Thelma Nobles, from church. He is taking her out."

"Well, I think that's great. "

"The woman is a gold digger, Jane. If he marries her, neither of us will get a *thing*."

"Thelma Nobles is not like that. Besides, she has money of her own."

"Jane you are *so* naive. This puts a whole different picture on things.

"Verna, can't you see the bright side just once? Let's be happy for Daddy that he's got a friend."

"She's more than a friend! I can tell you *that*. Calls him "honey," and talks about going off on a trip with him."

Jane smiled. "He hasn't even mentioned it to me."

"I wouldn't know it either if I didn't live here and answer the telephone three times a night, which is about the number of times they talk. That's on the nights they don't see each other which is about four times a week!"

"Well, this does sound serious."

"I *told* you!"

Then Jane's voice turned soft. "Verna, what is it you fear in this? Is it that he won't need you now? Or that you will lose the house? What is it?"

"I don't fear a damn thing. I just want what belongs to me."

Jane came back from the door and sat down. "First of all, they are simply seeing each other. Daddy would tell us if they had plans to marry."

"I'm saying we better think up something before he *does* tell us. Cause that day's coming, no doubt about it."

"Think up what?"

"There are papers people sign, I've read about it, that say a marriage will not change an existing will."

"Oh, Verna. You make me *so* tired. Just let the poor man enjoy himself. If things get serious, then we can talk to him and see what his plans might be in the event of a marriage."

"I'm telling you, the woman has woven a spell. He doesn't know whether he's coming or going, much less what his "plans" are. And unless we do something now, it could be too late."

"Do *what*?"

"Get her to sign a paper, that's what. Saying the will will stay as it is."

Jane let out a long sigh and shook her head. "I have to get home."

At the door, she turned and said as if the thought just came, "Thelma will probably be planning something for Daddy's birthday, herself. . . ."

"Probably making the cake right now," Verna said with a sneer.

"Well now, that would relieve you, wouldn't it?" Jane answered.

"They might even be going out to dinner. So don't plan on coming over here."

"I *certainly* intend to bring him his gift!" Jane told her, slamming the screen door. Then said over her shoulder, "You can just call and let me know the best time."

Verna quickly followed as far as the porch steps.

"If she takes his *name*," she said loudly as Jane was walking toward the car, "*everything* will change." When Jane kept on walking, Verna said louder, "It all hinges on the *name!*"

Jane kept her eyes straight ahead and opened her car door.

"You wait and see!" Verna yelled. "You just wait and see!"

Four days went by before Verna called to say that Thelma Nobles had invited all of them to her house to celebrate the birthday.

"Are you going?" Jane asked.

"Yes, I'm going. I want to see how this woman lives."

On Saturday, a little after five, Verna walked hesitatingly up Thelma Nobles' pathway, giving the house a close eye. She noted the size—medium, ranch style—and saw that it seemed in good repair and that the grass had been recently cut.

Her father opened the door like he lived there already, which galled Verna right off. When she walked into the living room, Jane and Bob and their two kids were laughing over something Thelma had just said, and that galled her even more. Late afternoon sunlight streamed from three, tall, drapeless windows, spilling orange and pink rays into the room. Verna squinted.

"Verna, do come in!" Thelma said, getting up. "We were just talking about your daddy being so funny yesterday at the store."

"Daddy can be pretty funny," Verna said with a scowl, and sat down.

One of the kids came over and hugged her, and she smiled slightly. But immediately afterward, a big shaggy dog came in wagging his tail, and quickly lured the children—who whooped with delight—into the den to play.

"Rusty loves children," Thelma said, then glanced at the clock on the mantle. "Oh. I better look at that roast."

"Let me help," Jane said, following her out of the room. Within moments the scent of pot roast, freed from its lid, wafted from the kitchen.

While Bob and her father chatted, Verna checked out the pictures in the room. It seemed Thelma had a pretty big family, and they were displayed everywhere. Couldn't squeeze another photo in this room if you tried, she said to herself. She noted a plaque on the wall with the words:"Best Grandma in the World." Somehow she had not figured Thelma with a family of her own.

"How are you, Verna?" Bob asked from his chair in the corner.

"Not complaining," she said.

"Well that's a switch!" her father said, and he and Bob laughed.

At the table, Thelma included the children in the conversation, and they were clearly quite charmed by her. Then when she brought out the cake they all sang happy birthday, even Verna, though her lips barely moved.

Later, back in the living room, one of the children came and sat next to Thelma, and put his head on Thelma's shoulder. It was a gesture generally saved for Verna.

Verna thought now was definitely the time.

"I've not seen the rest of your house," she said to Thelma. "Would you show me?"

"Of course," Thelma answered, kissing the child on the top of his head and getting up.

Then they were alone in one of the upstairs bedrooms and Thelma was telling what a time she had, trying to match the colors in the bedspread with the curtains. "But the pillows did it," Thelma said. "They brought the whole thing together."

Verna looked at the splash of colors in the grouping of what she thought were entirely too many bed pillows for one bed. Might as well get it over with, she told herself. She cleared her throat, then rubbed her hand on the rounded part of the bed post.

"You and Daddy seem to be seeing a lot of each other, now," she said.

Surprised at the change of subject, Thelma turned and said, "Yes, we are."

"And I know you are getting on."

"I guess you could say that," Thelma said, smiling.

"Well, we, I, was wondering if you had plans to marry?"

Thelma looked at her seriously. "Oh, Verna we have talked of it, but no date yet. And certainly you and Jane would be the first to know." Sensing Verna wanted to talk, Thelma sat down on the edge of the bed.

"Well, I think being as Daddy has a family already, you all might want to leave things as they are."

"Leave things?"

"Well you know, Daddy has a will as I am sure you do, too. And Jane and I are provided for in that will."

"Oh, honey, you don't have to worry about that! Goodness I am well provided for by my late husband. I wouldn't want to jeopardize anything for you. Or Jane."

Verna cleared her throat again. "What I am trying to say here is that there are legal papers for this kind of thing."

"I don't understand."

"Legal papers. Before a marriage. Signed. So that nothing is changed."

"I see."

"So we thought, I thought, this would be the best way," she said, rubbing the post again, absently.

"I see."

"Then it's settled?"

It seemed a long time before Thelma answered Verna.

"It could be that we won't even get married," she said. "It could be that things might get too complicated. Let's just wait and see." Then she led the way back downstairs before Verna could close her mouth.

The energy in the evening shifted. Thelma seemed preoccupied, and the kids got cranky.

Even the dog tired and went off by himself. "Please don't feel you need to help," Thelma said to them. "I don't mind the dishes."

"That's cause she's got me," their father said cheerfully.

When Verna heard his key in the door shortly after she got home, she went downstairs with a questioning look on her face.

"Thelma didn't feel so good," he told her. "Wanted to be by herself, it seemed."

Now when Verna answered the telephone there was no light banter, just, "Is your father at home?" And they stopped seeing each other so often during the week. When they did, it was always at Thelma's house.

Verna waited for her father to have it out with her, but the time never came. She surmised that Thelma had not told him of their conversation.

Jane invited everyone to dinner at her house a few weeks later, but Thelma made some excuse.

Finally, Jane came over one night, while their father was out.

"Yes, it's me, Verna," she said at the door. "And we need to talk."

Verna opened the door and went directly back to the sofa where she had been doing some hand sewing, and watching "Who Wants to Be a Millionaire."

Jane turned off the TV and sat down across from Verna. "What did you say to the woman?"

"I simply asked if they were going to get married, and she said it might get too complicated. 'Let's just wait and see,' were her very words."

"Things seemed to be so good, with both of them," Jane said, then paused. "You didn't say anything else?"

"No," Verna said in a flat voice.

Jane looked as though she doubted Verna's answer, but only remarked, "Well, give this to Daddy. Might cheer him up a bit, he seems so sad." Then handed Verna a bag of cashew nuts—his favorite—and went back home.

A month after that, Thelma stopped phoning at all. And Daddy stayed home, more often than not. And after another month it was as if the whole thing eased off without comment.

Now Verna cooked her father's special dishes, although he didn't eat much these days. And she didn't even put up a fight anymore over which programs to watch on TV, but rather waited until he decided, though he never seemed to be really watching. If she commented on the program—as they often had in the past—he would turn and look at her as if he had forgotten she was there.

A year later he had a stroke and Verna became the caretaker she had always claimed to be, although now it was true.

Once she saw Thelma Nobles in a department store. Verna was coming down the escalator, taking the steps by twos, hurrying to get back before the once-a-week physical therapist had to leave. When she saw Thelma, she stopped, one foot behind the other on the escalator steps. She noted the leisurely way Thelma strolled by the dress racks, then watched her hold up a colorful suit in front of the mirror and smile. As if she had all the time in the world.

Hattie

Hattie Dunn knew everything there was to know about everybody on Fleming Street. She had a careful way of looking just over her glasses—without moving her head or stopping the slow back and forth of the front porch glider, or even the clicking of her knitting needles—so that no one ever suspected they were being watched. Sometimes the knitting was replaced by a bowl of green beans, which she snapped in just the same careful manner, her eyes periodically roaming over the top rim of her glasses.

She knew Mildred Sommers was having an affair, had seen the man slip up the steps every Wednesday night when Jesse Sommers went to his Lodge meetings. She also knew Mr. Coverdell, who lived alone, had lost his job in the shipyard, and that two sisters on the block had a hard feud going over something quite silly. She knew, too, that Dorine—who had filled out much too quickly—was seeing a boy her father strictly forbade. And she knew other things, things like the time the police car brought Otis Brown home drunk.

Hattie's strong curiosity was a curiosity in itself. She had never asked a lot of questions as a child; the why and how of things had never stirred her, rather it was the movements of ordinary people she pondered, even pressing her nose into windows one summer until somebody told her parents. She had been a shy child in school, preferring to stay behind at recess to peek and poke in her school mates' desks. And as she grew up, her adroitness at eavesdropping became amazingly tuned.

She was not unattractive, but there was a plainness about her that stemmed more from a lack of interest in makeup and hairstyles, or clothes of the times. This plainness even aided her deeds of stealth, by giving her a form of camouflage.

There was one boy—Charlie Stamp—who asked her out. In fact, they almost had a thing going, but her incessant curiosity slowly turned on him like a high beam flashlight, causing him—after too many probings—to finally shout, "What *difference* does it make! Who *cares!*"

She became a teacher, but didn't go too far away. And after her parents died, she moved back into the house and ended by teaching English at Bryce School in the neighborhood, where the children's themes on family life had fanned her curiosity even more. Now she was retired.

All the houses on Fleming Street were of the same two story, narrow design, and so close they almost touched. There were no front yards—brick sidewalks came right up to the front porch steps—though the backyards were ample. The street, also narrow, brought the houses even closer, making it easy for Hattie to see the comings and goings of the occupants. And what she didn't exactly see, she imagined. It was better than anything she could read in the paper, which she had stopped taking anyway, being increasingly bored by the happenings beyond Fleming Street.

But this long time habit tripped her up one soft, quiet summer night when she slipped out on her porch, opening the screen door ever so softly in the dark, to better hear the argument the Hopsons were having on the porch next door. Avoiding the creak of the glider, she sat down on the straight back chair in the corner, drawn to the voices now raised a decibel, mesmerized in the dark stillness.

"Why did you *do* it?" Lilly Hopson, asked, her voice climbing.

"Because . . . I had to," Charles Hopson said simply.

"You never considered the children or me . . . not for a moment!"

"You don't understand," he said sadly.

She was crying now. "Staying out, *practically all night*!"

"Lilly, Lilly, I'm sorry."

There was a long pause. The lonely sound of the shipyard whistle blew in the distance.

Then he said in an imploring voice, as if he *so* wanted her to hear him carefully, "Lilly, did you ever experience something so beautiful . . . so incredible, that you wanted it to last forever?"

"No! Nothing would ever be that compelling to me!"

"You're just angry. You don't mean that."

Hattie heard Lilly Hopson get up and go into the house then, slamming the screen door behind her. She saw the dark silhouette of Charles Hopson sitting immobile for a long time. Then she saw the tip of his cigarette playing like a firefly around his face.

Not daring to go in until after he did, Hattie continued to stay on the porch, her eyes now drawn to a window across the street, where the shadow figure of Mildred Sommers, undressing, played against the shade.

"Rabbits!" Hattie whispered to herself in disgust.

Wednesday night of that week, Hattie saw a tall, dark-haired man knocking on Mildred Sommers' door. And though she had never seen his face, this time she studied the stance, the posture of the man, very carefully. She had never considered it could be someone in the neighborhood, but now she was sure this man standing in the shadows was none other than Charles Hopson. When he entered the house, Hattie closed her mouth, and let the upstairs curtain fall to its original position. She thought to herself, *If Lilly Hopson knew exactly who the woman was maybe she could put a stop to it, before things got really out of hand.*

Hattie made an appointment with her minister to get his approval first.

"If a family should be about to come apart because of . . . one person," she asked him, "and you knew about it . . . well, shouldn't you do your best to see that the information got to the right party?"

The minister, not a man given to nuances, and just about to leave for a meeting, said, "If I am understanding you correctly, you know something that would benefit a certain family?"

"Yes," Hattie answered. "A family in my neighborhood."

"Well, then, tell it!" he said. "We all need to look out for our neighbors. And good for you for doing so!"

Later, Hattie pondered how she would tell Lilly Hopson that Mildred Sommers was the one with whom her husband was having the affair. She was having a terrible time deciding just how to do it. Finally, she decided to write an anonymous note and put it into their mailbox that very night. She typed the note—only a few lines—and slid it into their mailbox at one o'clock in the morning. Then she stopped to sit on the porch a few moments in the dark, to catch her breath and still her pounding heart. Suddenly she thought to herself, *but what if it wasn't Mildred Summers after all, but some other woman?*

What if I were mistaken? Just then, she heard voices next door, and jumped.

"Shut the door quietly," Lilly told him, we don't want to wake the children."

"Come with me," he said, and led her to the bottom of the steps. "Now look."

"It *is* a beautiful night," she said.

Hattie saw him put his arm around his wife as they both stood, looking up at the stars. A full moon illumined their raised faces.

"This is what I was trying to tell you. The night I didn't come home . . . was such a night as this. Only it began with a shooting star, and then when I saw Venus rising, so bright, so incredibly bright, I couldn't leave. I had been reading about Mildred. . . ."

"The star. Mildred the star?" she said.

He corrected her. "The asteroid, rediscovered just last week."

"Yes. Mildred the asteroid," she said softly. "It was in the paper."

I had gone out to a clearing with my binoculars. And suddenly a world of things seemed to be happening up there! And I knew that very particular sky would not show up again in my lifetime. He paused and raised his head. "Just as this particular sky, will not come again, in ours."

Hattie lifted her own eyes to the sky, then.

"It's the *mystery* of it all, that draws me Lilly. The sheer, God-given mystery."

"I'm sorry I thought otherwise," she said, putting her head on his shoulder.

"No woman could ever take your place, Lilly. You should have known that."

"You always were interested in the stars," she told him.

He drew her closer. "Remember the night I proposed?"

"Yes. You had taken me to Ellis Field to see that comet. And you were so excited after seeing it."

"Not nearly as excited as when you said, *Yes.*"

"I love you, Charles."

"And I love you, Lilly. I always have."

Hattie Dunn waited until they went in and locked their door, before she went quietly and retrieved the note from the mailbox. A deep sadness came upon her, and as she walked up her steps there was a heaviness in her movements. She turned back momentarily and looked at the sky. "Mildred," she whispered. "Mildred the asteroid." The street was all dark now, except for the one light in her bedroom, upstairs.

Later, when she lay in her bed, she turned her head to her window and looked out at the sky. A tear fell down her cheek. In all her years of living alone she had never felt so lonely. But she didn't turn her head away, rather her eyes stayed fixed on the stars.

And from that moment, her watching shifted from Fleming Street to the sky. She brought a chair from the front porch to the middle of the backyard where no tall trees impeded the view, and where the surrounding fence blocked out all but the sky, giving her her own private planetarium. There she traced the path of Orion, rejoiced over falling stars, and there a meteor shower took her breath one night. And her ears, long tuned to eavesdropping, now heard only the night owl, or an occasional dog baying at the moon, as she sat immobile and transfixed, looking up at the sky—at all that brilliance, all that mystery. All that love.

Luther

Some things you just had to do, before things got done to you. And I had to see Dedi, one more time.

I revved up the old truck and took off down State Street. Where it deadends, I took a right, and when I was almost there I slowed up and parked the car, a little ways down the street from the old apartment house. I sat there for a while, just thinking about it, waiting for Dedi's mama to go to work. She always left first, now that she was on day shift at the diner. Seemed everybody in the building left before Dedi, who worked in a department store which didn't open until ten. Pretty soon, I saw her mama walk out the front door, and I slunk down in the seat as far as I could go. I knew better than to show my face until after that woman was gone. That was one mean mama. Last time we spoke there were few words between us, and those few were like lit fire crackers.

But now, Dedi—Dedi was sweet. And I had loved that sweetness for a long time. My court case was coming up tomorrow, and I knew if I could just see Dedi—if I could just hold her, hold her close, one more time—they could put me away forever.

"No account," her mama would say to Dedi, "He's no good," she'd say, with me sitting right there in the room, "Don't you see it. don't you know it!" she'd yell. And Dedi would look down, but not say a word back.

One day I asked her, "Why do you hate me so much?"

"You know why," she told me. "You're no damn good."

She didn't mind drinking my beer, though. If I left some in the refrigerator, she'd swig it down in a minute. Dedi didn't like beer.

Finally, I sat up a bit and tried to look over the steering wheel. As soon as I was sure she was gone, I smoothed my hair down in the rear view mirror, opened the door and got out. "Okay, Dedi, here I come," I said.

When Dedi came to the door, she still had on her bathrobe. She looked pretty as could be, hair all mussed, with that sleepy look still in her eyes. I knew she had at least a couple of hours before leaving for work.

"Oh, Luther," she said, "You know you shouldn't be here."

I just pulled her close, and said "Sugar, you know why I'm here."

It took us all of about three minutes to get in the bed. And all of about five more for Dedi's mama to come back and slip her key in the door. By the time Dedi and I were just going at it, she charged into that bedroom like a wild bull, jerked the bedspread off both of us, and stood there mad as hell.

"I knew you'd be here!" she yelled. "I had the feeling *too* strong."

Dedi screamed, "Mama!"

And I just said, "Jesus." It was then I noticed she had a gun in her hand. "Jesus Christ," I said, jerking the sheet up over my privates.

"Last time you're gonna see my daughter," she yelled, "Last time you're going to see anybody's daughter!"

I started talking fast then, "Look," I said, "they're gonna put me away tomorrow. I'm not going to see anybody's daughter again for fifteen years. You understand? Dedi will have herself a husband and a couple of kids by then. I just wanted to see her, one last time. You can't kill a man over that. You can't kill a man just cause he wants to see the sweetest daughter that was ever born in this world."

She softened a bit after that last part, about Dedi being the sweetest daughter ever born. But then her eyes turned cold, and she held the gun even tighter.

"You made a mistake coming here, Luther," she said. "I *told* you to stay away from Dedi."

Dedi was up, crouching in the corner by now, pulling her bathrobe tight, whimpering and crying, saying, "Mama, mama, don't do it! Don't do it, mama, don't *do* it!"

I just figured maybe my time had come, but I was going to try to talk her out of it, if I could. My heart was beating like crazy.

"I been smitten by Dedi ever since we were kids," you know

that," I said to her. "You know we went to school together, played together."

"Why didn't you leave her alone!" she said. "You didn't bother her in school."

"No, we were friends. I loved Dedi, but we were just friends."

"Yeah . . . you waited 'till she filled out, that's what you did."

"No, I waited until she wanted me. I never wanted any woman, unless she wanted me, too."

"God knows why she wanted *you*. God knows, I never saw it," she said. She raised the gun now. Sun made the handle shine. I knew she had started carrying a gun in her purse back when she worked the night shift at the restaurant, but somehow I had never pictured her using it.

"Mama, he's going to jail, tomorrow. Don't you *understand*? Leave him alone!"

"He'd be in jail right now, if his sister hadn't bailed him out," she hissed. She turned and looked steady at Dedi. " I *know* what's going to happen, Dedi. He's gonna get off like they all get off. That's what's going to happen. And he'll wait a couple of days, and he'll be right back over here in your bed. That's what I know. And your life's gonna be pure hell. Pure misery! Don't you see that?"

That made me mad. "I got plans, old lady," I told her. "I got big plans. Dedi would have a good life with me."

"Now just what are your plans, Luther?" she said, smirking. "What kind of big *plans?*"

"I'm getting me a ranch. I'm getting me a ranch with some horses, that's what," I told her. "I'm making a *name* for myself."

She laughed then, but the hand holding the gun stayed steady. "Making a name! Yeah, you'll make a name for yourself, all right." She laughed again, harder.

"You wait and see," I told her. "Even if they put me away tomorrow, I'm still going to do it. Jail ain't taking *my* dreams."

She was still chuckling. "What kind of money you gonna buy this ranch with?"

"Don't you worry about that."

And as if remembering now, she said, her voice more serious, "You hid that money, didn't you? You think it's going to be there when you get out." Then her eyes opened wider as if the idea just came to her. "Where *is* that money?"

"Mama, the other guy took the money. Don't you remember!"

She leaned closer, across the bed. "Where is that money, Luther?"

The police already looked everywhere for it, you know they have, Mama."

Her eyes were pure steel, now. "You might as well tell me, Luther."

She was a crafty old gal, I could see those wheels turning. I smiled then, real slow, just to aggravate her. And quick as lightning, she shot me in the foot. It felt like I'd stepped in a bucket of fire.

"Damn it, old lady!" I hollered, and Dedi screamed.

"Where is that money, Luther?"

"You crazy bitch, I don't have it!" And I didn't. For all I knew Charlie could have thrown it in Sewell's Creek.

This time, she shot just beyond my ear. I could almost hear the bullet whizzing by. Dedi screamed and lunged toward her mama, and I tried to get out of the bed. All I could do though, was put my legs over the side—I couldn't stand up for the pain. I just stayed that way, sitting on the side of the bed.

She shoved Dedi away, saying, "You want the same thing? You want the same thing, Dedi!"

At this point, I figured I had to tell her something—that it didn't matter what I told her, just so I told her something, and I yelled out, "I got a place in the wall. It's hid in there."

"You better not be telling me no lie," she said, her voice low and mean.

"Ain't telling you no lie, old lady. That's where it is." Then I said slowly, "Only you need me to show you." She had never seen my place, and I could see her thinking hard. She didn't even know where my place was. Blood was all over the bed.

"Dedi, tend to his foot," she said.

Dedi came over and knelt down to look at my foot. Her blonde hair was back-lit from the sun. She looked up at me, and all the compassion in the world was in that sweet face. She took my foot in her hands and held it, still looking at me, but with tears in her eyes now. Then she tried to wipe some of the blood away with a portion of the sheet, so she could see the wound better. I always did bleed like a stuck pig.

We both saw that it was only the big toe that had been shot, and though it took most of the nail and the tip end of the toe, it looked as though the bullet was not lodged, but had grazed. It would be our secret. Dedi left the sheet over the foot and got something to put on it, some antiseptic or something, and wrapped it quick with gauze. I pretended to be dizzy and fell back on the bed. Dedi pulled my legs back up on the bed, and covered me waist down with the part of the sheet that was not bloody, and I closed my eyes. For a minute, I savored being in that bed, Dedi's sweet bed. I was some kind of tired. By this time, Mama was sitting down in a chair, but still held the gun. I could tell this by opening my eyes just a sliver and looking at her through my lashes. I closed them all the way again.

"We got to get him on his feet," Mama said. "He's got to show me."

Dedi sounded tired, too. "Mama, remember how you used to say, 'Money is the root of all evil?'"

"*He's* the one needs to think about that," she answered. But I noticed even her voice sounded tired. Tired and old.

"Did it look bad, Dedi? The foot?"

"Not good," Dedi answered. And then said, "I don't know *why* you had to go and do that," and came and sat down on the bed, beside me, in what was probably the first act of defiance in her life. Even with my eyes closed I knew her mama's mouth was open.

I kept my eyes shut and Dedi rubbed the hair back from my forehead, in just the most tender way. "He even loved your cooking. Talked about it all the time, your fried chicken. Said it was the best in the world."

"I never heard him say that," she said, but I could tell her voice was softening—or else, she was still in shock at Dedi's attitude. "Oh, Dedi, what on earth draws you to him," she said sadly, and her voice had changed, as if she was about to give up.

"I don't know mama . . . it's just that when I'm in his arms, that's the only place I want to be."

I opened my eyes then, and drank in hers. There she sat, pretty as an angel. Maybe she *was* their angel. Maybe she was sent.

"I love him, mama," she said, simply, looking straight at me.

"And I love her," I whispered, closing my hand over Dedi's. "The sweetest . . . and the best child ever born to a woman in this whole universe," I said.

"You got that right," Mama said. Then her voice went soft. "Always did feel lucky to have her."

And in that moment I saw that honoring Dedi would make things right. I saw that it was *our* love of Dedi that would save me. Then I looked in her direction and said in a serious voice,

"You did good by Dedi. You did a good job." And then I laid back and closed my eyes again, as if I just couldn't stand the pain any longer.

"Lord, mama, what we gonna do? He's got to have some help."

There was a long pause. Finally she said, "You can take him somewhere to get fixed." Then she gathered herself up out of the chair and walked to the door.

"I'm done here," she said, like an old general who had lost the big one.

And then I saw—but it was like something flying by, I could hardly grab onto it, could hardly understand—that this, all of this, was all part of having to see Dedi one more time. That it didn't matter what they did to me in court now, that I, Luther Bates, had been redeemed. Redeemed by love and a shot in the foot.

General B.D. Martin

All the streets which formed the junction were named after generals. The most important one was named after General Pettyjohn, so it was called Pettyjohn Junction. It was a major intersection, an area you almost always had to go through to get to somewhere else. "Where the generals convene," is how it was often described.

Rumor had it that one of the street names—a general whose shady past had caught up with him—was going to be removed, and a new general would be so honored. Maybe, even, someone local. General B.D. Martin had high hopes they would pick him. His background was flawless. The only thing in his long career that might hold him back was his wife, Bobbi, who many considered had been a bad choice.

Bobbi often used the junction to get on and off the base, and was approaching it now, on the way home from shopping, in her convertible with the top down, tapping her fingers on the steering wheel to the singing of Aretha Franklin. She loved her convertible, loved feeling the wind in her hair, loved the freedom of it, which clashed with the restraint of military life. She always seemed to be repressing an urge to push her foot down harder on the gas pedal, and take off down an open highway to some unknown destination.

She had married the General because she had trouble with decisions, and making decisions was what he did best. When they met he was fifteen years her senior, and though not yet a general, certainly well on the way. She was flattered that someone so important was in love with her. But mostly she loved the way he made her feel, the way her hair sometime stuck to the side of her face, after they made love.

In the early years of their marriage she tried to do all the things expected of the wife of a man of high rank—albeit reluctantly. But for the last few years, she had let her real feelings come to the surface. "I don't care," she told B.D. last night. "My life is just that . . . mine."

He had been telling her to tone down again, watch her step. "Be careful what you say, Bobbi. People are listening."

"No, you be careful. You're the big cheese around here."

And he had looked at her with those steely eyes which always caused a twitch or two in the men under his command, but had little effect on her. "You are being watched," he said finally, his words firm this time, his tone serious.

As she entered the intersection of Pettyjohn Junction, she had to stop to let a convoy of trucks go by. She turned the radio down and became somber. She wasn't worried about being watched—she knew he had only told her that so she would be careful—but the seriousness of the faces going by in the big trucks brought her back to the reality of the General's position. She knew B.D. had a lot on his mind. I'll make him something special tonight, she thought. Maybe lasagna. It was Clara's night off, anyway, and it was one of his favorites.

Trouble was, she had a little too much to drink while she was cooking, and when the General came home he thought he saw her weave slightly when she opened the door. "You been drinking already?" he asked. For a long time he had feared she was drinking in the daytime and trying to hide the fact.

"No . . . well maybe just one," she said, kissing him on the neck and quickly turning toward the kitchen.

He would have belabored her statement, but he had just been told of a special assignment, and had exactly one hour to get his things together. He took the stairs by twos. "I've got to pack," he said over his shoulder, and she stopped short in the hall. She knew what that meant; he did not have to elaborate.

When he came down with his bag all ready, he stationed it at the door and called to her.

As she came to him, he said, "You cooked tonight, didn't you? I'm sorry." He was looking toward the kitchen. "Smells good."

"Lasagna. I put some in a container, for you to take."

He held her tight. "I'm going to miss you, baby."

"How long, this time?" she asked.

"At least a week . . . could be longer. I'll let you know." She sighed and leaned against his shoulder.

"Bobbi," he said in a serious tone. "Promise me you'll be careful of your drinking."

"You are always telling me to be careful of something," she said, and stretched up and nuzzled him on the cheek.

"No, I'm serious," he told her, pulling back and looking at her face—the only slightly faded prettiness, the mischievous smile, the tinted blond lock over one eye. "You need to watch it," he said, but inside, he sympathized. He knew the prevalence of liquor on all the bases they had lived had fed into her weakness over the years. He had no patience with a man who couldn't hold his liquor—personally, he could out drink the best of them—but a woman, well, that was a little different. The way he saw it, it had something to do with their size. Still, he wanted to be sure she would be okay while he was gone. "People talk," he said seriously. "You need to be aware."

"Who cares? I'm not in the Army, you are."

He held her arm a little too tight, then. "Yes, you are. As long as I am, you are, too." Then he loosened his grip and gathered her against his chest. "I'll be gone a while, this time . . . try to . . ."

"Behave myself?" she said, slipping her fingers under his collar, softly rubbing the skin on the back of his neck.

"Yes," he mumbled against her hair. Yes . . ."

"I wish . . . we had more time," she said, her voice slightly lower, almost a whisper.

He glanced at his watch, took a quick look out the window, and frowned. "The car is already here," he told her. "Got to go, baby." Then he kissed her goodbye, gathered up his suitcase and the container holding his dinner, and hurried out to the waiting car at the curb.

She stood at the window, watched the driver salute and take the suitcase, and then watched them take off. She stood there until she couldn't see the car anymore, then went back to make herself another drink. But when she got to the kitchen, she found herself standing very still, listening hard to discern whether the sound outside the open window was a squirrel in dry leaves, or someone moving.

The town was almost a resort when nothing big was going on, its proximity to the beach, a noted river and other waterways, and its seasonable weather, drew an array of tourists. But when something was going down—cold or otherwise—everything changed. It all leaned too far in the other direction. The two bases woke up like hives after a long, cold winter, buzzing with activity. There was the noisy sound of big battleships getting ready dockside, the thunder of jets overhead, the whirring of helicopters on maneuvers, and, sometimes, the rumbling of equipment being moved out of the underground weapons depot. Only the subs moved out quietly, slithering into the water at night. Everything teemed with a singular focus, rendering all else in the city secondary.

Bobbi had known both peace and wartime in the area. She especially remembered the Persian Gulf War; remembered those "getting ready" times as if yesterday. There was always a dustiness at first, as if items generally stored were being shaken out, like taking sheets off the furniture in a house normally unoccupied. Though she had heard of nothing specific, it felt like that now to her—as if something out there was getting ready.

"How're you doing, hon?" he asked the first night he phoned.

"Big Brother is alive and well in Dodge."

"What's that supposed to mean?"

"I mean the videos that have been put up in certain areas of town, especially Pettyjohn Junction."

"Videos?"

"Supposedly to catch people running a light, but we all know it is mainly to keep an eye on things."

"How many at the Junction?"

"One on every corner of the intersection. It's crazy, B.D."

"Nothing is crazy, if it's done to protect," he said.

"Yeah, yeah."

"So . . . what have you been doing?"

"Painting a little." She didn't elaborate.

"Good!" he said, thinking it would keep her busy. And keep her hands off a glass.

Actually, she was kind of excited about the watercolor she had begun that morning—a peaceful landscape with a covered bridge. It wasn't great shakes—she had not painted in a long time and it was mainly a hobby, anyway—still, it pleased her. But there was something about the bridge that bothered; everything else worked in the painting, but she couldn't quite get the bridge. On her walk that morning it came to her, and she stopped to sit on a bench and write, *Take out the bridge*. Then she put the note into her jacket and went on.

It was a beautiful day and she paused to watch a family of herons, perched on two logs in the small lake which ran the length of the trail. In a moment one of the herons raised its wings high, and then folded them back, like a fan had suddenly been opened and closed. Bobbi smiled and raised her own arms high and then lowered them, as if greeting the heron. Shortly, the heron raised its wings again, this time keeping them there. Bobbi raised her arms and left them in the air, too. She waited until the heron lowered its wings, to put her arms back down. Afterward, when she turned to go she noted a man, a military type in jogging clothes, doing stretching exercises a short distance down from her, on the bridge. She had seen him earlier and knew that he had been there just as long as she, and that was a good while ago. As she walked by him she noticed he broke his practice, and followed. No stretching exercises took that long, she said to herself, hurrying on. He is watching me.

That night, she remembered the note she had written regarding the bridge, and took it out of her pocket and looked at the words. She laid the note near the painting, to remind herself in the morning to delete the bridge. She thought of the soldier, the one who had watched her in the park. What if she had dropped the note, and he found it? Would he think she was a spy? Then smiled, remembering how she had greeted the heron with her arms held high. Would he think that was a secret code sent to someone on the other side of the lake?

When B.D. called her later, she told him of the incident and laughed. But he didn't take it as funny.

"You always do things a little differently," was all he said, visualizing her in a public place, raising and lowering her arms to a bird.

"Yeah, B.D., I'm different from the good folks," she said, swishing the ice around in her drink.

He heard the ice and winced. He wished there were someone he could call to come and stay with her, but she had no close friends. It had always been just the two of them. And even Clara was home now, with a sick child.

"What's your schedule this week?" he asked. Normally, she had to do a fair amount of entertaining, or at least sit in on meetings.

"All clear. Miracle of miracles, all clear," she said. Actually, she had canceled two occasions in her book, but was not about to tell him this.

"He tapped his fingers on the night table thoughtfully a moment, frowning. "Well, you have your painting. . . ."

The next day Bobbi had a headache and stayed in bed longer, and when she did get up, found she wasn't in the mood to paint. The house was too quiet without Clara's bustling about, too big and quiet with just her in it. Normally, the phone would be ringing—a staff member telling her about last minute details for some luncheon coming up, or someone advising her on a topic for a meeting with the officer's wives. But she had canceled all that, at least for this week, and did not miss the incessant ringing. The house, though, was much too quiet. She decided to go shopping. Inside the store, she put a maroon sweater up to her face and looked in one of the long mirrors, to check the color against her skin. But, instead, her eyes were drawn to the corner of the mirror where she saw a man in uniform, standing not ten feet away, watching her. She frowned, threw down the sweater on the display case, and walked out of the store, furious.

"They are watching me!" she said to the General that night when he called. "What did you do!"

And after she told him about the shopping, he said, "I didn't do anything. You are probably watched because I'm being considered—just considered, mind you—to be one of the names at Pettyjohn Junction."

She let that sink in, then said, "What's that got to do with me?"

"You're my wife. They want to be sure you behave like a General's wife."

"No . . . I don't think that's it, at all. No, somebody's stalking me, B.D."

"Stalking is a pretty strong word. Don't be ridiculous."

But later, as he dressed for a dinner where the vice-president would be speaking, he pondered the situation, wondering if maybe they were carrying it too far. It was true, because of the drinking he had told two people on his staff to keep an eye on her while he was away. But although he did not like to acknowledge it, there was still another reason. Though she had never given him any cause not to, something deep down inside him didn't quite trust her. She was too beautiful. Even now. And too much woman.

There was always an undercurrent of secrecy during normal times—who was being shipped out where, and so forth—but in a time of war the atmosphere could get somewhat paranoid. Even someone taking a simple photo of a sunset down at the river could cause concern, if a battleship happened to be in the background. But, actually it was the ones who had too much information in their heads who often were the biggest concern. Because there was always the fear that somebody could get this information, if they perceived an

Achilles heel. So all associates were watched closely, and in some cases, even family members. Bobbi was keenly aware of this fact.

"It clicked, a couple of times, like somebody was messing with it," she said the next time he called. "I heard it, Daddy."

It was the first time she had called him Daddy, in years. He rather liked it, though he knew it was fear not endearment that brought it out now.

"I'm telling you, the answering machine clicked. Really loud."

"Now, Bobbi . . ."

"You know what I think . . ." she said, "I think somebody is trying to get my messages before I can take them off."

"They would have to have the code to that particular machine, before . . ."

"No, it's not like it plays back messages when a code is used. Just two loud clicks, that's all. Like something is being zapped."

"No one can do that," he said in an even voice.

"Sure they can! I know it, and you certainly know it!"

Reticent to say anymore, he changed the subject. But that night he lay sleepless, with his arms behind his head and his eyes to the ceiling, thinking. They were carrying it too far, but he was reluctant to stop it, just yet. He had heard only today that his name was in the forefront for Pettyjohn Junction. He would be home, soon, anyway. He'd just wait until then to curtail it. The next day, Gen. B.D. Martin took his place in the reviewing stand to oversee one of the most outstanding troops in the nation. It was times like this that made him proud, made him feel the full sense of his vocation, made the medals on his chest rise. Of course this was peacetime; in times of war his vocation fueled him. While he stood looking over that huge field of khaki, he began to see—just a flash in his mind's eye—his name on a street sign at Pettyjohn Junction. He thought of Bobbi, and hoped she would not sabotage his chances. When he first married her, he had thought she would be amenable to military life, and as moldable, perhaps, as his men. But she had turned out to be the only part of his life he could not predict.

He spent the whole of the next day discussing highly classified information with both military and government, subject matter experts. It was unsettling news they had brought, and he and others were going to have to come to some sort of agreement on how to deal with it.

That night when he called Bobbi, she started right in, breathless, something about an ice cream truck stopping near the house again, "Second time in two days . . . just sitting there," she told him. "Two men, just sitting in an ice cream truck."

"Now, you can't be concerned about a simple ice cream truck," he said, rubbing his forehead. The all-day meeting had exhausted him. The threat of terrorism—the focal point of the meetings—was more serious than he had thought. None of his briefings in the past had pointed this strongly to what could happen right here, in the U.S. Anytime. The whole day had left him wanting only a drink and quiet.

Normally, he liked to hear her voice; it was soothing to him. But tonight her voice was grating. "And they stayed almost half an hour, B.D," she said, her voice climbing higher. "Both times!"

"Bobbi, Bobbi. . . ."

"That truck could contain listening devices," she told him. "Could be a front."

Before he could stop himself, he said sternly, "Straighten up, Bobbi."

There was a long silence. Then she asked sarcastically, "Is that an order?"

"Yes, goddamn it, that's an order!"

She just waited, as if waiting for the words to die down. Finally she said in a voice so quiet he could hardly hear her, "That hurts my heart, Daddy."

He put his head in his hand, and rubbed his forehead over and over. The last thing he wanted in the world was to hurt her. "I'm . . . sorry," he told her now. "You know I didn't mean it. I've . . .just had one hell of a day."

She was quiet for a long moment, then said, "I'm tired. I'm going to bed now."

"Sure . . ." he said. "You go on, hon. Get a good night's sleep. Maybe that's all you need."

But before she hung up she said softly, "Somebody is always watching somebody. Even you. And you know what, B.D.? Even the President, I bet." After another long moment she said, "Ever wonder who is watching the watcher?"

When he put the phone on the cradle, he sat and stared at it for some minutes. Then he fixed himself a large scotch and water and took it, and some paper from his briefcase, over to the desk. Tomorrow was his day to speak, and what he had been told on this particular day would change everything he had previously planned to say. These were heavy times, so many things were possible, so many hot spots in the world. Anything could happen. In the past, after he had been given a briefing on serious matters like this, he found himself looking around at the general population at large, spotting them all dressed up, going to some party, some gathering, laughing in their cars, and would think, *They have no idea*. But he lived in that world, too, making polite conversation at his niece's wedding, or a godson's graduation, attending a baseball game, making love to his wife. He often felt as if he lived two entirely different lives, and was constantly battling to keep them balanced. He envied the ones who relied on their religions. Envied their little yearly rituals—the ashes, the talk of resurrection, the cross—which seemed to give them some sort of answer, that though aware of the devastation that could be out there at any moment—floods, hurricanes, sudden deaths—gave them a cushion, a way to cope, a way out. That kept everything at bay. He had no rituals. Except with Bobbi. Bobbi was his sacred cup, his shrine, his way out. His life.

At that moment he was remembering how badly he had wanted his name on a street sign at Pettyjohn Junction, and it sickened him. The thing was so paltry, compared to the importance of the talks this week. He picked up the pen and began making notes for his speech. A strategy was the thing, he thought.

Throughout his whole life strategy had played an important part. He even had a strategy when he asked Bobbi to marry him. Though thinking back now, he couldn't see how she could have refused, they had sparked so definitively from the start.

What he had to do, was convince tomorrow. Convince a roomful of politicians that a rumor had to be taken as seriously as the real thing—particularly if it revolved around possible terrorism in the very near future. And particularly, if the information came from a valid source.

"And you shall hear of wars and rumors of wars . . ." Where did that come from? Churchill? Or is it biblical? Maybe that's what I'll start off with, he thought.

When he finally got to bed, his mind was swarming with all the day's voices, especially the last, "Even you," he heard her soft voice again, just before going to sleep. "Even you."

The General left for home the next day, right after his speech. He had no idea what effect it had—other than his hand being shaken quite vigorously afterward. Only time would show the real results.

On the plane, he was struck by how much he wanted to see Bobbi. No other woman had ever made him feel as she did, and he had been with plenty, before their marriage. He was thinking now of how she loved to rub her hands over the hair on his chest, calling him *My big teddy bear*—sometimes burrowing her face in it. It made him close his eyes and swallow, and lean back a little in the seat. He realized then, she was the only human he had ever allowed himself to get close to—not his family, nor even anyone in the military family, in all these years—living as if in a code. The thought was sobering.

He looked out the window at the sun sparkling on the army insignia on the partially cloud covered wing of the plane, then half-closed his eyes to the lulling drone of the engine. All the others . . . all of them, he thought, they were just on the periphery. But, Bobbi . . . she's the one who cracked it.

Six months later, a sign bearing the name "General B.D. Martin" was erected at Pettyjohn Junction. As it turned out, the pride that would have gone to the General circumvented to Bobbi. It served not only to tamp down her drinking, but also to view her station—the wife of a general whose name was so honored—with a more composed manner.

Not all of her complied though. She took up painting again, this time with such passion one local critic cited, "The large, bold strokes and explosive colors seemed almost too much for their frames."

Maxwell and Jerome

When introducing himself, Maxwell Porter always emphasized his last name by accenting the first syllable. Por'ter, he would say, Maxwell *Por*ter. And some slight trace of supposed importance would hang in the air.

Early on, he had decided that some things needed to be emphasized to get where one wanted to go. Take clothes, for instance. Maxwell favored a tweedy, casual look, and took great pains to see that his tie, when he wore one, was the telling accent—the thing that went just a bit further to say, if the sweater and jacket had not quite done so, that he was a man of taste. The ties were more works of art than garments, their subtlety of color and design blending perfectly for that overall, impeccable look Maxwell so desired. He also emphasized his vocation. He was never just an account executive with one of the largest companies in town, but "I handle the Pharr account. Yes, I'm with Thompson and Row."

His best friend was Jerome Richards, a man of similar aspirations, who was also with the same firm. Often they had dinner together at Paul's, one of the better restaurants in town. The only thing they ever seemed to argue about was either the selection of wine, or whether to get the special of the evening or go with one of the selections on the menu. By now waiters knew to leave them be, and come back much later for their order. But once past the ordering, they settled in for a rehash of work-related incidents of the day. Soon, usually by the time the wine neared the bottom of the bottle, the conversation always changed to Phyllis.

"She is showing signs of . . . something else now, you know?" Jerome had changed the subject.

"What?" Maxwell answered without bringing his head up from the *Confit d'Oie*.

"Well . . . she is dressing differently, now. More provocatively."

Maxwell stopped chewing and looked at Jerome thoughtfully.

"Yes, I've noticed that."

Jerome continued. "Those soft blouses, with the top button left undone."

"Yes." Maxwell looked away, and began chewing again, almost as an afterthought.

"And polishes her nails. I've never known her to do that before."

"You're right!" Maxwell said, pointing his knife for emphasis, "Never!"

"She even walks differently now. I was behind her today, walking toward the water fountain. The way she moves . . . like a lioness. Shifting from one side to the other . . . so slowly."

"So deliberately," Maxwell added.

"You have noticed, then?"

"Oh, yes. The walk, I've noticed."

"Who do you think it could be?" Jerome said, at the same time complimenting the wine—his choice—and taking another sip. Both men had secretly hoped to make an impression on Phyllis, but she had, at all times, maintained a rule of not dating anyone with whom she worked.

"Well, no one at T&R, that's for sure," Maxwell said.

"But who then? She never speaks of a man in her life."

"Maybe we are wrong . . . maybe there is none."

"No, I feel sure of it. Something's changed," Jerome said, "Something has definitely changed."

The next time Maxwell and Jerome got together for dinner, they did not even argue over the wine, nor bring up office politics, rather got right down to it. "Mussels," they both agreed, quickly closing the menu. But Maxwell had to add—not to disappoint the waiter who always seemed to note with pleasure each wine selection they made— *Gros Plant*. The waiter nodded and smiled.

"She looks awful! Coming in like that . . . like someone in a daze, her hair still mussed!

I thought she'd been up all night," Maxwell started.

"She doesn't even say a word to the women. They know no more than we do." Then Jerome lowered his voice. "When we get back—and I could be wrong, certainly—but look at her eyes. I detected a blueness under one, as if, maybe . . . she was slapped."

"Surely not!" Maxwell exclaimed.

"Well, just look, if you can. And see what you think."

The next time they did not even order, having no time for menu deliberations. Instead they asked the waiter for straight scotch and water, and got right to Phyllis.

With great agitation, Jerome began, looking down at the table-cloth and shaking his head, "I still can't believe it."

Maxwell loosened his tie, something he almost never did in a public place. "It's incredible. She was so very beautiful."

"I . . . even thought . . . hoped, one time, that she would go out with me," Jerome said, looking up sheepishly.

"Yes, I guess we all did."

"Do you think she actually went to that place . . . that sleazy place, with him?"

"That's what the police said."

"But the bastard could have made her go, couldn't he?" The waiter had come back but Jerome waved him away.

"The police say she had been seeing him for some time. They even found a note that made them think she was, indeed, in love with him."

"I don't understand it. To fall for someone like that!"

"She didn't know his background, of course," Maxwell said.

"No, of course not," Jerome echoed.

"It's a dangerous thing . . . relationships," Maxwell said.

"Yes," Jerome agreed.

They finally tired of talking about the sad fate of Phyllis. One night a beautiful woman walked slowly by their table with that same deliberate, lioness stride—halting their forks in mid-air—and as they watched the woman walk out of the restaurant, it was as if Phyllis, herself had walked out of their lives.

But the enigma remained. And soon they were discussing other women, and even men, who had made unwise choices. Sometimes they discussed Steve Wainwright, the head of the department, who was known to take full charge of any office situation, while at home deferred totally to his five-foot-two wife. It was all so perplexing to Jerome and Maxwell—this obsession, this sheer power of love. "Surely control plays some part in one's life!" Maxwell would say.

They talked of these things safe within the confines of restaurants, as an occasional pianist played and sang soulfully about this same obsession. The words floated by their table, the turn of a phrase sometime even causing them to pause a moment. But then they would play with the words in some superficial way, Jerome asking, "Why is it love is so often associated with a rose?"

And Maxwell's answer would bring them back.

"Because the thorn is sure to prick in the end!" And they would laugh, some safe distance now from the very real torment they had seen on the pianist's face as he sang. To be able to end their evening knowing that they, themselves, had escaped this malady, put a lightness in their steps as each went home.

Sometimes they went to museums together, always standing just a bit too long, a bit too pensively, in front of certain paintings or sculpture of beautiful women. And it was not as if they had no women in their lives—quite the contrary. A succession of women came and went. But always there was some flaw, which Maxwell and Jerome, of course, discussed at dinner.

"I couldn't possibly have lived with that kind of attitude," Jerome would state.

"No, of course not," Maxwell agreed.

"It just wouldn't have done! We are . . . too different, that's all."

"Yes. I saw that immediately."

They always managed to get out just in time, managed to stay that safe distance away from all that emotion and despair they knew must be out there. Just waiting for them to succumb.

They saw themselves like the "smart bombs," keeping all that face-to-face combat at bay.

Brody

Brody Hawkins was the best ballplayer Jennings high school ever had. Best pitcher, anyway. Whenever he was out there winding up that long arm, no hot dogs were sold, and nobody ever got up to go to the restroom, and all you could hear was "Brody, Brody, Brody!"

One spring, just about the prettiest spring Jennings, Alabama had seen, a lucky breeze blew in on Thomas field and lit right on Brody's shoulders. Later a journalist would describe the moment:

All the lights seemed spotlighted on Brody Hawkins in the last few minutes of the game, and there was an unreal hush in the stands when he began that slow, deliberate winding. Strike one! The crowd roared. And then that steady gaze and the body's perfect contorting once more—Strike two! The crowd roared louder now, and that fluid body—loosed from the young man to some muse—was doing every-thing right, going beyond even Brody Hawkins' wild expectations of himself. Strike three! And the crowd exploded. Then the fireworks started at the very moment Brody's teammates lifted him up on their shoulders, and paraded him all around. Ah, the sheer wonder of it all. What a game!

People knew something extraordinary had happened, but no one could put it into words.

Even years later, after all the speculation, nothing was ever really defined. But the ones who had been lucky enough to be there that night, never tired of talking of it.

"That was the night Brody Hawkins. . . "

But Brody, himself, well, that was another thing altogether.

Seems as though he never was able to get beyond it. It was as if time changed for him, after that night. It started first with Evie, his long time girlfriend. After that wild explosion, though she was included in all the celebrations she felt a kind of wall beginning, as if the fans were not going to let anything—or anybody—come between them and their hero. And it was not so much the fans, even, that slowly pushed her away, but Brody himself. Or the Brody he had become after that one fantastic game.

It was almost as if he had become someone else, someone who saw himself with keys to doors that went far beyond the town of Jennings. Yes, he, Brody Hawkins, was going somewhere, he told himself, no doubt about it. And who knows? Maybe there will be other girls—*lots* of different women. Better give myself some room, he thought.

Even his folks—ecstatic for two whole weeks—began to see the difference in their son. Never having to be asked to take out the trash or mow the grass before, now Brody had this reply, "I have *other* things to think about now, mother. *Important* things."

His father, who was living out his own failed baseball days through Brody, agreed.

"The boy is going places . . . leave him be."

Scouts came out of the woodwork after that night, fanning Brody's ego even more, making promises of offers to come at the end of the season. Big promises. Trouble was, they were still watching. Waiting to see if Brody could deliver again, or if that particular night had been a fluke—a one time thing. And as they waited and watched, that fortuitous breeze never again settled on Brody's shoulders. And the crowds in the stands—once adoring—turned hostile. The home-town boy had betrayed them, couldn't live up to the gift. Even his father's wide grin turned sour.

It would have been better if he had never known that frenzied moment, that incredible night. Because now he had nothing. No girl (she had since got engaged to Tommy Brent), no more offers, and his mother heaped more chores on him than ever.

When his friends went away to college, he stayed home. He had counted on a baseball scholarship, and when that didn't come his family could not afford to send him.

He got a job at Charlie's Auto Repair, and finally married Sue Turner whose aspirations more or less matched his own. They had a couple of kids and lived a good, if uneventful, life—the only vestige of that special night being the roar of the crowd, shouting his name, which he heard most nights just before dropping off to sleep.

Then all of it came back when he received the invitation to his tenth high school reunion.

As he dressed for the dinner/dance, he looked into the mirror and slowly began to see himself in his old baseball uniform, with his father standing just behind him, beaming, and heard the crowd again cheering, *Brody, Brody, Brody!* Then the image began to fade as Sue walked into the room.

"Are you going to wear *that?*" the old Brody said to Sue when she stood before him in the new dress bought especially for the reunion. He recognized his mistake the minute he saw her face, but didn't have time to right things now; he was going to see the old gang, and needed to hurry.

When they arrived at Stanford's, where the dinner and dance was to be held, the old Brody completely took over. He deposited Sue at a table beside another couple, and went happily in search of the old team, his chest out, shoulders back, a big smile beginning to break. When he saw Joe Wilson approaching, his smile spread further—but, funny thing, Joe walked right by him. Brody turned around, "Hey, Joe!" he yelled. "Joe!" Joe Wilson looked back then, and threw up a hand, "Catch you later."

He saw several of the old team members around the bar, and made his way toward them.

Instead of the "Look who's here!" he had expected, he found the circle almost impenetrable, and the conversation intense.

"The guy was innocent. I knew it . . . that's why I took the case," Paul, now a lawyer, said.

Sam, presently running for mayor, replied, "My constituency doesn't think so. And, frankly, I don't either."

"Well, you're wrong, Sam. And you better get your facts straight before you run against him."

"Hey, guys!" Brody said, sidling up to them.

"Hello Brody," Paul said, then turned back to Sam, "I tell you this for your own good, Sam."

Then, after a pause, the two men looked at Brody. "What you up to these days?" Sam asked him.

Later, when the band played an old favorite, Brody sauntered over to Evie and asked her to dance. When she followed him out to the dance floor, he took her in his arms and gave her that old one-sided smile and half-lidded look that had once mesmerized. She looked back with a steady gaze and asked, "How many children do you have now?"

Walking back toward his own table after returning Evie to hers, he noticed the balloons were not as bright, and that one of the letters in the sign on the stage was crooked.

"Brody Hawkins!" someone called out, and Brody turned to see Mrs. James, who had been his music teacher. He went over to her and she stood up and gave him a hug.

"Stay a minute," she said, then introduced him to her husband, a large man with a genial smile and firm handshake. "This is the one I told you about so many times," she said to her husband.

Brody could feel it coming now, the first wave of it about to crest. The man was obviously trying to remember and Mrs. James said to his perplexed face, "Brody Hawkins, *you know!*"

Brody relaxed, it was going to be a good night, after all. He knew that at any moment the man would jump up and pump his hand again, harder now than before, and say something like, "What a play, what a perfect play."

But it did not happen, instead, Mrs. James, one hand on her hip in exasperation, said, "The boy who couldn't get the hang of the tuba!"

Mr. James laughed out loud then, "This one?"

"Yes!" she said.

"Oh, that *was* funny," he said, and was still laughing as Brody walked away.

Mrs. James' questioning face followed Brody.

"I didn't think he *cared*," she said, sorry now at her choice of words. "He always made such jokes about it . . . even said he only took the class because it thought it would be easy." Then, as if still trying to excuse, she said again, "He made *jokes.* . . ."

Mr. James had turned all around in his chair, still watching the departure.

"Seems there was something else about that boy," he said now. "Didn't he play baseball or something?"

When he got back to Sue, Brody suddenly remembered the dress. "You know . . . you really look nice tonight," he told her. And when he danced with her he held her especially close.

Sue went quietly upstairs while Brody took the sitter home. When he returned, instead of going on to bed, he went down the hall and tiptoed into his son's room.

Moonlight from the window fell on some things left on the floor, and Brody leaned down to pick them up. He put the little shirt over the back of a chair, and returned the few toys to the chest in the corner. Then he gently pulled the covers up on the boy's shoulders, and patted him softly.

Going into his daughter's room, he smiled at the ménagerie surrounding her, leaned over the various dolls and stuffed animals, and kissed her tenderly on the forehead.

Later, lying in bed, he realized something had changed. The roar of the crowd often present just before sleep, was receding now, becoming fainter and fainter, until finally he heard only the even sound of the breathing of the woman who lay sleeping in his arms.

It was this that mattered, he thought. This was what was real.

Savannah

Savannah Brown was a woman who always knew where she was going. And had no doubts that she would get there. She started out slowly, but once the caffeine kicked in, she was off and running, and look out Central City.

If she was asked to get the real skinny on the Mayor's latest mishap for instance, she not only knew—by the end of the day, even—he was going to campaign against funding for the arts, but that he had a woman on the side, as well.

Her strong, willful streak—which first showed itself in the stamping of little feet as a child—had served Savannah well as a journalist. But her most valued asset was an uncanny ability to draw out information. She had a way of asking questions that did not seem an intrusion, rather genuine interest, and people told her things—sometimes outrageous things, even information a therapist might have spent years trying to unearth. She also had a way of saving the "big" question until just the right moment; her timing was perfect. A natural talent, her peers acknowledged enviously, as they stood a little distance from their own stories, never being allowed that up-front closeness that Savannah Brown took as her rightful place.

But when the great pianist and composer, Hemmel Brockmore, came to town, things changed. Affable enough on stage, once the concerts were over he retreated, surrounded by his trusted staff, and granted "absolutely no interviews."

Ever since she had been given the story—"If anybody can get it, Savannah can"— she smiled and talked her way past all the people who surrounded him. But she knew the real barrier was the man himself. Was there something in his past, she wondered, some secret shadow, political perhaps, that made him shy away from interviews? She stayed up nights thinking out and writing down questions on her yellow tablet, honing, getting everything just right for the moment she should find him receptive. Because that moment would come. She was sure of it.

Once, she caught his eye as he hurried out of the hotel, his tall frame towering over the surrounding ménage. Another time, she smiled at him as he was being ushered into the back door of the concert hall, and he smiled back. She heard him play that night and was overwhelmed by the sheer range of talent and velocity.

She sent a note the next day.

"Last night's concert was masterful. It would be so interesting to see if the man's mind matches his fingers." Then added, "You know, interviews are generally granted in America."

Finally, the breakthrough came. He sent word that he wanted to have dinner with "that determined young lady."

Savannah's boss was ecstatic. "Now, here is what you ask him." he began, but Savannah waved the idea away.

"I've got it. " she told him, "in here," she said, pointing to her forehead. "So don't confuse me."

Hemmel Brockmore sent a limo for her at seven. He was to meet her there, the driver told her, the great man was "practicing."

"I'm to take you to Harold's," the driver said. Savannah knew the upscale restaurant well, also knew it catered to celebrities who wished to be left alone. The driver turned and said to her with his eyes still partially on the road, "Arrangements have been made, the maître d' will seat you."

Savannah walked in like she owned the place, in a black dress that foretold every move, its neckline just low enough to be interesting. She had picked out her very best earrings, which gave off moving light under the piled up hair. Under normal circumstances, she was a woman of confidence, but now, gathering even more strength from the heads turning her way—here and there, and over there—she was a woman of power as well. The maître d' smiled, and when she gave him her name her perfume caused him to lean down a little closer, as if he had not quite heard.

She had only a short wait until Hemmel arrived.

There was no apology. "You look lovely," he told her, taking his place at the table.

"Thank you."

"Well. Here we are."

"Yes."

"What are you drinking?" he asked as the waiter appeared.

"Scotch."

He smiled. "I would have guessed a more ladylike drink. But then, you are different, are you not?

"I don't do it to be different," she said. "I like scotch."

"Of course," he said, smiling.

He gave his request to the waiter, and Savannah marveled at his good English. She attributed it to his father, who was British, although she also knew from research that Hemmel Brockmore had lived all his life in Germany, his mother's birthright.

When the waiter left them, the great man looked straight into her eyes. "So Savannah Brown, what made you decide to be a journalist?" And from that moment, it was as if he had stolen her gift; as if he were the one skillfully extracting information. As if he were the first class journalist, not she.

They talked all through dinner. Suddenly she realized that none of her questions had been answered, rather he had turned them all back to her own life. She wasn't even sure she had asked the main questions. In fact, right now, looking at his face, that lazy smile, those powerful eyes, she didn't really care.

It was only after the limousine had brought her home—after first dropping him off to get in another hour or so of practice—and she was sitting at her dresser taking off the earrings, that she looked at her image and said, "You know what? You've been hoodwinked."

At the office, she only said, "I'm still working on it. I don't want to talk about it now."

In the middle of the afternoon, a member of his staff called, and then handed the phone to Hemmel. He mentioned a special dinner he would like to take her to.

"As my guest," he said. "You'd enjoy it. Some very interesting people will be there."

She let some time lapse, fingers still posed on computer keys, the phone cradled on her shoulder. "I don't think so," she said, finally, surprising even herself. "We've done dinner. Let's do walking." Then suggested they take a walk on the beach on Saturday. Walking, looking straight ahead, she would not get so caught up in those eyes she told herself, she would be able to gather her thoughts carefully, not let him get the upper hand this time.

He laughed and said, "All right, I'll send the car around in the morning."

"No," she told him, "I'll meet you there."

"You want to drive yourself?"

"We keep our space this way," she said.

Saturday was an Indian summer day; a sky brushed with white, haphazard strokes, rather than clouds. At first she had trouble finding him—they were to meet near the pier—but then she remembered his celebrity would demand a disguise in such a public place. When he walked up to her in a floppy straw hat and dark glasses, she laughed out loud.

Once barefoot and adjusted to their own paces, and after a few lighthearted comments and sightings of special shells, she began to probe. But the sound of the ocean and the squawking of the seagulls drowned out her questions. She stopped walking, finally, and looked out over the water.

"What is it?" he asked.

"Let's sit a moment, she said, and walked away from the crashing and the birds, near one of the dunes.

And she gathered up all her resources, and the one question, the one that would break through, was waiting in her throat when he turned and looked at her. He had taken off the hat and sun glasses, and looked relaxed and comfortable. His eyes were as blue as the sky behind him. She got caught up in all that blue, and the question in her throat faltered, came out puny, causing him to ask, "You don't really care about that, do you? You don't want to ask me *that*?"

And the question tucked its tail and slunk back. He put his hands on either side of her face and drew her closer. "Savannah. Listen! The ocean is saying your name, over and over. Listen." He kissed her then. And the sound of her own name whirled around and concentrated, like a seashell had been brought to her ear, *Savannah. Savannah. Savannah.*

She never got her story. But after he went back to Germany, he composed his best symphony. And if one listened very carefully, the sound of seagulls could be heard in the horns, and the swell of the ocean in the strings. A music critic in Berlin called it one of his best compositions—"A romance of the highest order."

When Hemmel sent her the CD, her colleagues often heard the music coming softly from the door of her office, on late afternoons. And afterward, when she emerged, they found her pace slowed, her demeanor changed.

"Mellowed," one ventured.

She told someone she had got the story, afterall.

"It's all in the CD," she said.

Ruben

Ruben had a dark, slippery side, but it was hidden under impeccable manners and a way of listening that endeared him to most of the women he encountered. He slipped into one town or another—it didn't seem to matter to him—wrecked some havoc, and then slipped out as easily and covertly as a dark bird taking flight at dusk.

In New Orleans, he took money from Phyllis. Oh, she gave it to him all right, but it was his slick-talking that prompted the turn of the wall safe.

In Atlanta, it was Sally's fine Kutani vases. "Take them, love, you admire them so," she had told him.

And in Dallas, he managed to squeeze a couple of oil wells out of Doris.

But when he got to Memphis, Carlean had his number right off.

In the beginning, it was her walk that attracted him. He had seen her crossing a street and simply followed a couple of blocks, until she turned toward the entrance of a restaurant with bright, green awnings. It was that pause at the window—pursing her lips, reading the posted specials of the day—that prompted him to have lunch early. That, and the way the sun sparkled on the diamonds in her large dinner ring as she lightly traced a line of the menu through the glass. "Allow me," he said, opening the door for her.

He waited until after she was seated, and then requested "The table by the window, please." Hers was only a few feet away.

He made a point of choosing the chair nearest her chair, and smiled as he sat down. She smiled briefly and opened her menu. The sleeve of her jacket slid back, just enough to show her watch, which was, he was sure, a Presidential Rolex.

He glanced over the menu, and then looked up. "I was told the sole is quite wonderful here," he told her.

She looked over at him. "I don't like sole," she said.

"Oh?"

"I'm getting number eight," she said, and looked away, as if looking for a friend.

When the waiter came, Ruben listened carefully to hear if she might mention waiting for someone, but she simply gave the man her order.

The waiter stood at Ruben's table next, and began the recitation of the specials of the day. Ruben held up one hand to stop him. "I've decided on the sole," he said.

The restaurant had a slightly European atmosphere, and there was some sort of background music, classical in intent, which was not unpleasant. It was up just enough to keep conversations private.

"I wonder," Ruben began, "if you could possibly tell me how to get to the Conner building? I have a board meeting this afternoon, and need to get my bearings.

She looked at him very carefully. "A board meeting?"

He smiled. *It was working already.* "Yes . . . this one is pretty important, and I wouldn't want to be late."

She hesitated a moment, still looking at him quite carefully.

"Oh, I'm sorry. Excuse me. The name is Ruben. Ruben Roberts."

He always used an alias. He had been Ruben Cunningham (the cardiologist), Ruben Hamilton (the bookseller), and Ruben Zuskin (the jeweler). But he always kept his first name.

"The Conner Building is just around the corner," she said slowly. "Almost directly behind this restaurant, on State Street.

"Thank you," he said. "That sounds easy enough," then looked away, as if it had simply been a question, after all.

"I'm curious," she asked. "Who is hosting this meeting?"

Smart. Just like I like them, he thought. Savvy. "The Conner Corporation," he told her.

"Really?" Her eyes grew large.

"Yes. The Coke people are flying in, and CEO's from some of the largest companies in the country. I'm sure it will be in all the papers."

"Interesting. Very interesting."

"It's going to change some things . . . once this product catches on."

"And the product is?"

This is one to keep on your toes with, no doubt about that. "It's pretty much top secret," he told her, "for now."

"I see."

"But the media will be alerted, soon."

"Of course."

Shortly, the waiter brought the dinner tray, and began serving her table.

Before she picked up her fork, she ran one finger thoughtfully under her wide, gold necklace. "Roberts, you said?"

He was surprised at the interest in his name. Usually that didn't happen. But he had detected something different in this woman . . . some undercurrent. It was just under her words—and he was a keen listener.

"Yes. Ruben Roberts. Here . . . I'll give you my card."

She looked at it and smiled. "You are a physician, as well?"

He quickly took the card back. "Well, I was . . . a doctor. Heart surgeon actually, but had to give it up. I started getting cramps in my hands, and of course, that wouldn't do."

Her smile spread. "No," she said, "I guess not."

"Here is my present business card," he told her, offering again.

She was well into number eight by now, and only nodded in reply, and left the card on the corner of the table.

He decided on another tack. He took out a cell phone from his attaché case and pretended to put in a few numbers. "Charles," he said, his voice taking on an air of importance now. "It's Ruben Roberts. Do you have those figures for me?" He paused, then said with authority, "Well get them!" The waiter was standing nearby, waiting to put down his plate. Ruben nodded for the waiter to proceed, and continued talking, his voice becoming a little louder. "You know, of course, these figures will make or break the meeting. They are of *utmost* importance. Call me the minute you have them." He put the phone back, loosened his tie, and sighed. Then turned back to her.

"Sometimes the responsibility is enormous," he said.

She smiled and he thought he detected a bit of humor in her eyes, but took it for mischievousness. He loved that trait in a woman. He took a few bites of the sole, and out of the corner of his eye, noted her looking at the card. He knew the title would intrigue.

"So. President of . . . Finance and Fortune?" She dabbed the corners of her mouth, the napkin just covering her smile.

"Yes," he said, in a tone that seemed to give his answer the needed gravity. "It is a very large concern."

She quickly dabbed the corners of her mouth again, and held the napkin there, a moment longer than necessary.

He was quietly finishing his meal, waiting for her to say something. He was sure she would. This pause, this expertly timed pause, was where they all said something, gave some indication of interest, often offering to show him a bit of the city. Though he didn't look up, he could feel her eyes, knew she was looking at him.

When she didn't comment, he said, "I usually stay a while when I come to Memphis. But it can be quite lonely.

She finished the last of her coffee, took one look at the Rolex, and rose.

"You're leaving?" His eyes were incredulous. But she was rising, adjusting the shoulder strap on her pocketbook, already pushing her chair back in, his card left on the table.

"You're actually leaving?"

She leaned down then, and whispered as if to a confidant.

"I actually am."

He watched her walk a few feet away. Then as if an afterthought, she turned back to him. "You know, I didn't introduce myself . . ."

Here it comes, he thought. I knew it. She is going to give me her phone number.

"Carlean Conner," she told him. "My late husband was Jay Conner. I took over as President of the Conner Corporation when he died." She paused and gave him a large smile. "Enjoy your meeting," she said, then hurried on as if already late for something important.

Ruben picked up his attaché case, noting for the first time it was beginning to show signs of wear. He got up slowly and headed toward the front desk with his check.

I should have seen it coming, he said to himself.

Oma

Oma Thomas had lived the better part of her growing up years in an orphanage, and that one fact had opened a myriad of lives to her. Not knowing who her father and mother were, she could be—in her mind, at least—anyone.

Shortly after she received a scholarship and went off to college, her roommate fixed her up with a blind date.

"Where are you from?" the roommate's friend asked as they walked toward a pizza place, just blocks from campus.

"India," she answered, which made him stop and stare a moment.

"You don't look or sound like you came from India."

"No, I went to excellent schools." And my parents were English.

After they walked on a bit, he said, not without some awe, "I guess . . . that gave you a whole different outlook?"

"Oh yes. I see things in a deeper way," she said.

But later, when she found herself getting too caught up in answering questions about India, she never dated him again. A little bit of India remained, however, giving Oma that whiff of mystery that some girls take years to cultivate.

When she gave an oral report in her English class, she said she was descended from a long line of lighthouse keepers. My great-grandfather stayed out there—two miles from land, all alone." Then, when she knew she had their rapt attention, she focused on Jimmy Turner's long legs, which sprawled into the aisle, and slowly brought her eyes up to his, saying dramatically, "Silence was his friend."

Afterward, Jimmy followed her out of class. "Your great grandfather . . . the one who stayed out there all by himself . . . he must have really been *something!*"

She gave him an enigmatic smile and nodded. "He loved the ocean," she told him, especially when it crashed up on the sides of the lighthouse," and then added, "He had no fear."

They went out a number of times but Oma never got him off the subject of lighthouses, and soon tired of all the questions—some of which exceeded her original research for the paper and left her floundering for answers. It was just too much.

One of the hardest things in her memory was being left, when people would come to select a child at the orphanage. They would see her sullen look, and pass on by quickly. She was always thinking, *I don't need you . . . my mother was a princess.*

Once, in a fit of curiosity, she went back to the orphanage and asked for her records. One of the nuns told her there were none.

"We simply opened the door one morning," the nun said, ". . . and there you were in a little basket, wrapped up in a soft blanket with no note. For your last name, we gave you Thomas, after the saint, and then chose Oma for the sweet sound of it."

When Oma looked down, the nun lifted her chin with her fingertip.

"We often thought the mother would contact us over the years, but she never did." Then noting Oma's sad expression, added "But the basket was very clean, as were you. I imagine she was quite young, and most probably, scared."

The story did not deter; rather fueled Oma's imagination even more.

Often, in the college library, Oma's eyes would slide away from the page and the scene she had just read would be recreated on the library wall like a movie, only now she was the star player. She could literally see herself in any book. Currently, she was Anna Karenina and already she could hear the train coming.

Had she become an actress, it would have saved her. As it was, she majored in business—something to hold onto when her imaginary life threatened to become too real. When the four years of college were up, she went to work for Martin and Bloom, and after only six months became office manager.

Things clipped along; she even managed to make a little money in the stock market. But then she made the mistake of telling someone she had been an opera singer, who passed this information on to

Mr. Martin—an opera buff—and the whole thing began to collapse. Mr. Martin remembered her résumé citing Cincinnati, a town he knew well, as her home. "Did you sing in Cincinnati? he asked, when they met at the water fountain.

"Oh, yes. For many years," she told him, "My father was also an opera singer."

"Really?" Mr. Martin had lived in Cincinnati for years and had attended every opera produced. "And his name?"

She paused, not expecting this. "Peter Hudson."

Mr. Martin just stared, wrinkling his forehead. When Oma realized what she had done, she said quickly, "His stage name. Of course his real name was Thomas."

Mr. Martin had never heard of Peter Hudson.

"What operas?"

"Madame Butterfly, for instance. I loved doing that one."

"No, your father."

"Oh . . . well I remember Tosca . . . and . . ." But before she named another opera, he asked what part her father had played in Tosca. She looked quickly at her watch.

"Excuse me, Mr. Martin, I just remembered a call I need to return."

When he continued to ask opera questions of her every time they passed in the hall, it became painfully obvious that she was lying. And it all went downhill from there.

She had as much trouble with men as she did jobs. She became engaged to Bill Peterson, a vice-president at the new company, only a year after she changed jobs.

She told him she had lived in Africa for some years, where her father was head of a large diamond company. Told him of going big game hunting with her father, and of swimming nude on some of the most "incredible beaches in the world." Bill Peterson found her fascinating. And actually, the more she described Africa, the more she began to believe it herself—as she often did when she told something so convincingly. But when holes appeared in her story, Bill Peterson began to back away.

"You are such an attractive woman, Oma," he told her finally, "But you lie all the time!"

Men came and went. Who could possibly measure up, she reasoned, "When I could be *anybody,* from *anywhere.*

So Oma never married, instead went through a succession of relationships and occupations, and any number of personas.

Once she took a meditation class which seemed to help. The chanting of OM turned into a form of her own name, her mouth forming the long Oooooo, then when going into the mmmmm close, adding an "a" just for herself.

Oooooommma. As if she were chanting her own name, as if she were combining all her parts into a whole. It tied things together in her mind. At least for the duration of the meditation class.

When she was old, she couldn't remember which persona to assume, and after moving into an assisted living home this proved an enormous source of entertainment for both the other residents, as well as herself.

"Now tell us again, Oma, just where you came from?" someone would say, with a wink to one of the others.

"Spain," Oma answered without the slightest pause. And with her chin up, her back straight, she'd do a little tango for them.

"Were you rich?" someone else said, ". . . or poor?"

"Very, very rich," she would answer, twirling. "You can't imagine the opulence."

Casey

Casey didn't get to be a cheerleader in high school, though all her best friends did. It was the first real disappointment in her life. And it was the one that stayed just under every disappointment that followed, from the university that turned her down on the lack of only five points, to the only man she ever really wanted, leaving town. The day Lloyd English left town, Casey went into her room and didn't come out for three days. The family came in great numbers to knock on the door, each one imploring her to come to her senses, but she would not answer them.

Finally, the youngest member of the family—a nephew she was particularly fond of and had often baby sat—came and whispered,

"Caphy . . . can you come out and play?" That at least brought an answer.

"I can't Billy Joe, my heart is broken." After a bit of quiet, the little boy whispered again.

"Can't you get it fixed?"

Casey was sitting on the floor, on the other side of the door now.

"No. No one can fix a broken heart," she said, leaning her head against the door.

He was trying to see through the key hole. His whispers came through the hole.

"Why did it get broken?"

"Lloyd English broke it."

"I hate Boy English."

"You don't know Lloyd English. And you don't hate anybody."

"Yes I do. I hate Boy English."

"It's Lloyd, not Boy."

"I don't care what it is . . . if he was here right now, I'd punch him out."

Casey smiled then, for the first time in three days.

"And you know what else, Caphy?"

"What?"

"I'd stomp on him. I would!"

She chuckled in spite of herself, and opened the door a crack.

"You don't want to do that, Billy Joe. You don't have a mean bone in your body."

Billy Joe put his nose right up to the crack in the door and looked in at her.

"Can I come in?"

"You don't want to be around me now. I'm too sad."

"I'm sad, too," he said, his eyebrows almost touching.

She looked down at the pathetic little face and opened the door then, and went back to her bed.

He came and stood by the side of the bed and rubbed his hand over the balls of the chenille bedspread.

"It's a *silly* name," he said.

"What?"

"That Boyd has a *silly* name." He plucked one of the balls so hard it almost came loose.

"It's Lloyd," Casey said. Then she sighed long and hard. "A beautiful name."

Billy Joe laid his head down on the bed like a big dog, and plopped his thumb in his mouth. Casey stroked his head absently, looking up at the ceiling.

"Mama said it was "cause of love," he said, then put the thumb back. Then he took it right out again and said forcefully, "I'm not ever gonna go near no love."

Casey sat up then and pulled him up on her lap.

"Yes, you are Billy Joe. Some little girl is going to turn your head so fast you won't know what happened."

"Then I'm not gonna go near no girl, either."

She held him close.

"Billy Joe, love is just about the best thing in the whole world, when it's right. It's what your mamma and your daddy feel for you. And it's what I feel for you, too. That's love that's good love."

"Well, I'm never gonna get no bad love."

"Get *any* bad love, not no bad love."

"I don't care what you call it. If it's bad, I don't want it."

Casey laughed out loud then, and hugged him. After a moment, she said, "See that letter over there, Billy Joe? Can you hand it to me?"

Billy Joe stretched out his little arm to the night table and retrieved the letter for her.

She sighed and opened the letter for the umpteenth time since she had received it. It was from the university and there was a note at the bottom which she read again now, with Billy Joe's head on her shoulder. *Although your SAT scores were not high enough to gain entrance at this time, you may take the test again at a later date and be reevaluated.*

Casey folded the paper and put it back in the envelope. She tapped it lightly on her hand, looking out the window.

"What you thinking about Caphy?"

"Studying. That's what I'm thinking about," she said. She took in a deep breath. "And trying again."

She got up and opened all the curtains, letting light flood the room for the first time in days. Then came back and kissed him on the top of his little head.

"After that," she said, smiling, tipping his chin up and looking directly into his eyes, "I'm going to look for some good love. And let that ol' bad love go."

Billy Joe's eyes brightened.

"And then can we play?"

Harna

Harna hailed from the back woods and people knew this before she said a word. Just the way she looked straight at you caused a conversation that might have turned funny to stay on the narrow path.

Folks never saw her in anything except jeans and denim shirts that spoke of catalog ordering, but she wore them with a style all her own. She never wore jewelry; all that unruly red hair proved ornament enough.

She was the only one left in her family, having lost them all one night in a freak auto accident—mother, father, and only living grandparent—coming back from a church meeting. That's when she took over the land and the apple orchard and moved into her grandparents' house in the woods. People worried about her living all alone out there. It seemed something hard had turned over in her, after the accident.

"Books are all the company I need," she told them. And after a while, they left her alone.

She had a country air attractiveness that caused men to turn around, but they always stayed a little distance, as if afraid of something. Except for Lester, and he followed her around like a dog. She let him do it as long as he didn't get too close. When that happened, she'd turn those steely green eyes on him and he would look down like a hound being chastised. Dubbed "slow" or "touched" by most of the town, Lester enjoyed a special protectiveness from Harna, and he adored her.

Harna continued to keep her distance from most of the townspeople, until a man named John Lucas moved into the log cabin up in the hollow. He didn't turn around like the other men when he saw her in the feed store, just nodded and went about his business. And this, of course, made her turn around. She'd heard he had been away for some years, and wondered if he was of the old Lucas family that moved up north, years ago. That name—the Lucas name—she remembered from her childhood. She had been on her grandparents' side porch, playing dolls in the sun, and stopped when she heard the normally soft-spoken voice of her grandmother rise higher and higher.

"Can't you get that Lucas family off your mind! What have they ever done to you?" her grandmother shouted, while Harna's head turned slowly toward the open window. Her grandfather had remained silent, but the name of that family and the power of it to raise her grandmother's voice had stayed with her all these years.

One afternoon, before John Lucas pulled away in his Ford pickup, she knocked on the window and when he rolled it down she asked, "I need a little help with these things. Could you give me a ride home? I walked and I've got these things."

Where any of the other men would have had some excitement in their answer, he simply nodded and said in a matter-of-fact voice, "Sure." and got out to help her put the heavy bags into his truck.

She saw two beautiful, hand-hewn chairs propped in the back corner of the truck. "Yours?" she asked, rubbing her hand over one. The wood was incredibly smooth. "You made them?"

He nodded. She had heard people came from all over to buy his furniture.

"That's what I do," he said simply.

"Three miles down, and turn right at the crossing," she told him after the truck got revved up.

They didn't say much. He seemed intent on driving and she was curious about the books he had moved over when she got in. She recognized two of them, she had them herself, but the title of the one on the bottom had her stumped. She had to turn her head sideways to read it. *A Modern Book of Esthetics*. It did not seem to fit with the large, work-worn hands on the steering wheel.

Finally, she said, "Didn't know Sam would get the order in so soon. That's why I walked."

"That's okay. I don't mind."

The window on his side was down and her hair, worn free, was blowing. He looked over at her. "Window too much?"

"No, I like it," she said, pushing her hair back, twisting it over one shoulder.

She caught him looking at her hair again and knew the sun, which she felt on her shoulder now, must be making sparks in the shine.

When he turned at the crossing, he kept his eyes straight on the unpaved, bumpy road, banked by undergrowth. The further he drove the more mysterious the land looked. Finally, he saw a small house in a clearing.

"That it?" he asked, and she nodded.

He parked the car in the turn around and helped her carry the things in.

"That's fine," she said, "just set them right there. And thanks."

He didn't look too anxious to leave. He was staring close at the picture on the wall.

"My granddad," she told him.

"I knew him," John Lucas said, then corrected himself. "I knew of him."

"How?" she asked, surprised at the bitterness in his voice.

"You don't want to know," he said, making his way to the door.

"But I do."

He opened the door and walked out on the porch. "It's a long story," he said, and walked on to his car without another word. She stood on the porch and watched him drive off, her mouth slightly open.

The next time she saw John Lucas she was riding one of her two horses hard, her long red hair flowing behind her. He was putting up a fence and didn't raise his head.

"Whoa," she said to the horse, and tried to catch her breath from the horse's quick stop.

"John Lucas." she called out.

He looked up, then.

"What do you know about my grandfather?"

"I know he was a mean son of a bitch," he said, wiping the sweat off his brow. "That's what I know."

"Well we all knew that," she told him.

He leaned down and began putting some things into his tool box. Then slammed it shut.

"I don't like talking about the man. He cheated my family out of some money."

And with that, John Lucas turned and headed up the hill, the tool box swinging in his hand.

Harna watched him with a frown on her face for a moment, then turned her horse around and rode him hard, straight home.

That night, Harna's eyes rose from the book she was reading and lighted on the old desk in the corner. The desk had been her grandfather's. She put the book down and went over and pulled up the accordion-like front. Then took out two ledgers and went back to her chair. Sometime after the accident she had tried to read through the ledgers, but had put them back when tired of reading seemingly unrelated figures. Now her eyes gave them a more careful and thoughtful going-over. For a while she just ran her finger down page after page, but when she finally found what she had been looking for, she took the ledger over to the table and adjusted the lamp directly over the page: 1934—Took over the Lucas property. Good timber.

Foreclosure.

There was a letter attached to this page, and Harna carefully took out the yellowed pages and read. When she finished reading, her eyes went from the letter to the picture on the wall. The eyes of the man in the picture seemed to be staring straight at her. She glared back.

"You *were* a mean son of a bitch," she said. Then she got up and removed the picture from the wall and put it face down in the desk, along with the two ledgers. She closed the roll top hard, then took a tablet and pen to the kitchen table and began to write. When she finished, she folded the sheet and wrote John Lucas' name on the front of it.

In the morning she took her coffee to the front porch and looked out. Her eyes scanned each tree that bordered the house.

"Lester!" she yelled. Lester!" And a figure slunk from around one of the trees and came to the porch steps.

"If you're going to hang around this place every blessed day you might as well be useful. Here, take this note down to the Lucas place."

When Lester just stared at her, she said "You know where it is, don't you?"

Lester's face showed how pleased he was to be asked to do something for her.

"Well, do you or not!"

Lester nodded his head up and down and came closer, to retrieve the note. She leaned over and put it into his shirt pocket, patted the pocket a couple of times, and smiled at him.

Overjoyed, Lester started off down the road, a little peculiar skip in his walk, rubbing the spot where she had patted him. Harna, still smiling, watched, shaking her head.

When Lester reached the Lucas place, he walked into the yard and up the steps cautiously. He knocked tentatively at first, then a little harder. When no one came to the door, he peeked around the back and saw John Lucas chopping wood. Lester walked over and handed him the note.

John Lucas read it with the sun behind him, his long shadow falling on the page and on Lester. When he finished, he looked just beyond Lester's head, as if no one was there, and crumpled the page hard in his big hand. He kept crumpling it, his face now as hard as the hand. Lester stepped back a little, as if afraid.

"Here," John Lucas said to him, holding the note out, his hand shaking with anger. "Take it back!"

Lester didn't move for a moment.

"Take it back!" John Lucas yelled.

Lester grabbed the note then, and turned and ran as hard as he could, back down the road.

When Lester got to Harna's house, she was outside filling the bird feeders.

"Well?" she said, when he stood before her. He didn't say a word, just put the crumpled note in her hand, and went on home.

Harna stood alone in the breeze, holding the note, the caw, caw, caw of a blackbird filling the air, and yelled out "You satisfied now!" But her anger was not directed to the crumpler of the note, rather to the man whose picture lay face down in the old roll top desk.

After that, John Lucas looked away whenever he saw her. This went on for some weeks, until one day Harna followed him out of the feed store and when he got a little down the road, she called out, "John Lucas, I want to speak to you."

He continued to walk on down the road. She thought him the tallest man she'd ever seen.

"John Lucas! I've got something to say!"

He turned then, and stared at her, without a word.

"There are," she began carefully, "a lot of apple trees on the old Lucas property. They are doing good this year and I want to share that yield with you."

"Look," he said in a hard voice, "you already told me I could ride or hunt on the property, . . . and I turned your offer down, remember?"

She didn't say a word, just stared at him.

"This is no different. I don't want your charity," he said and continued to walk on.

"It's not charity! It's common decency."

He turned back around.

"Your family should have thought about "common decency" a long time ago. It's a bit late, now."

"I can't be blamed for something my grandfather did decades ago!"

His eyes turned hard.

"Yes, you can," he said, and as if that finalized the whole thing, got in his truck and drove off as Harna watched, her fingers balled up in her hands.

That night, Harna sat at her dresser for the longest time, just looking at herself. Then she picked up the brush and began brushing her hair, over and over again. She had always known she was pretty, but it never mattered to her. Now she was curious about it. There was no vanity in it, just curiosity. She opened a drawer and took out a little velvet box. Then she removed the emerald earrings which had belonged to her mother and began to put them on, as lamp light ignited first one, then the other. At that moment she heard something at the window, and sat very still. When she heard the sound again, she reached down slowly and quietly and slid a pistol from the bottom drawer. Then fast as the wind, she sprinted to the door, jerked it open, and shot one time in the sky. The sound of the shot echoed in the woods. She shot one more time. Nothing competed with the sound except Lester running fast and terrified, through the woods.

Some time went by in which Harna and John Lucas did not even look each other in the eye, even walked across the street, if one saw the other coming. Once, while riding, he spotted her out on the same hill, and right away pulled his horse in the opposite direction. But the clouds that had formed earlier, had turned into one big, dark, swirling cloud, that seemed destined for the town. When John Lucas saw the funnel, he looked back at Harna. He was sure she had not seen the dark cloud, since it was behind her. He also noted she was riding away from the direction of her house. He looked back at the funnel cloud once more, then spurred his horse and rode quickly toward Harna.

"Tornado!" he yelled when his horse sidled up to hers. Both horses, sensitive to the change in the air, were skittish.

"What?"

"Tornado!" he yelled again, turning now and pointing to the dark cloud behind them.

When she saw it, she nodded one time and started riding fast, motioning for him to follow.

They were now riding on the old Lucas property, and John Lucas began to note the land. There was a ledge up ahead and she rode toward it, turning to wave him on. When she got off her horse, she led him to a cave-like area under the ledge and tied him close to the entrance. "Come on!" she yelled, and John Lucas came and tied his own horse among the semi-shelter of surrounding rocks, as close to the entrance as possible.

Once inside, he saw that the cave appeared to have been used. Harna picked up a flashlight near the front of the cave, and led John Lucas into the darkened area in the back. The light from her flashlight illumined a crudely-made bench. They sat and listened to the eerie sound of the wind, and even as far back as they were, felt its presence.

"I have candles, but no point in lighting them."

"Do you use this place often?"

"Yes," she said, and left it there.

He took the flashlight out of her hands. "Just to get my bearings," he told her.

He flashed the light down the sides of the cave, and the light lit on a cot on one side of the cave, and on the other side, he noted stacks of books and a lantern.

"You'll ruin your books," he said, "keeping them in this damp place."

"It's not as damp as it might appear," she said, taking the flashlight back. "They are okay."

A crack of lighting lit up the cave for seconds, and then the dark funnel seemed closer.

"Here it comes," he told her. "Hang on to me."

"I'm fine," she said. But when the horses began neighing, and a sound like a low rumble of a train in the distance grew louder and louder as if the train were loosed from tracks and running wild in the fields, she grabbed him tight.

He pulled her down to the ground level and lay over her, pulling his jacket up over his ears, shielding her as best he could. His mouth was touching her ear and though the roar outside was tremendous, she could hear him breathing. The cave was pitch black now. They lay like that, for some minutes, until the storm subsided. He let her loose then, and they both got up slowly.

When they went outside to check the damage, they saw many uprooted trees on the other side of the valley. The horses seemed to be all right, though still restless, pacing in place. Quickly they untied them, and mounted.

"Hope your cabin is okay," she said to him.

He nodded. "Your house, too," he said.

Then they rode off in opposite directions

Later, she rode up on the hill and looked down to see if his cabin was still standing, while he, at the same time, was driving his pickup down the old road to her house, stopping just short of the turn-around, to note no damage.

All spring he still kept his distance, and although now he would nod slightly, continued to look away when he saw her.

When summer came, she rode up to the cave for the first time since the tornado. It was a warm day and she tied her horse in the shade and went in. For a while she lay on the cot and read. But her eyes kept leaving the page, as if her thoughts were more important than the reading. She lay back and closed her eyes. She stayed that way until a long shadow formed, from the entrance. Then she opened her eyes very slowly, already knowing who it was.

Afterward, they sat on the cot in a daze. A hard rain had formed, though they were just now becoming aware. There had been no words, and none needed; they were two creatures in tune with nature and the land, who had simply come together naturally.

Now they sat quietly and listened to the rain, both still a little stunned.

"Wonder if our grandparents ever came here?" she said finally.

He was uneasy with the words and it showed on his face.

"They would have needed some secret place," she said, "to have an affair back in those years."

He made no comment.

She waited a moment, then ventured, "I found her letter to him in a ledger. It sounded almost as if she—they—had been caught up in a powerful passion."

"She married someone else."

"Yes, I know. And that's why he did what he did. The foreclosure."

He looked at her, his face hard.

"Took the house away from a young couple with small children who had a crop that failed." He had pronounced each word slowly and positively.

"Then the next year, *took the land!*" When he spoke again, his voice was strained. "My grandmother pleaded and pleaded and plead-ed with him."

"Yes, I saw that in her letter. She was desperate. 'For the chil-dren's sake,' she said."

"My father told me stories of going hungry as a child, of hearing his mother crying long into the night. He used to tell me all about this land, the apple trees, the mountains—how he had loved it so, as a child."

He got up then.

"My father was a very unhappy man. All his life. And I have hated your grandfather all mine." He looked at Harna seriously. "You and I . . . this can't happen."

"It's already happened," she whispered.

"Even so, he said, "it can't *really* happen," and he walked straight out of the cave.

While he was untying his horse, she stood at the cave entrance and said, "So that's it?"

"That's it," he answered, and got on his horse and rode off.

Harna let her temper out then. And while she flailed the surrounding trees with a fallen limb, her horse jumped and twitched as if there were still a tornado around.

In the fall, they both ended up in the hardware store at the same time. They almost ran into each other, down one of the aisles. He nodded and walked straight by her to the other aisle. But when he heard Tom Hardy's voice asking her about the things she was buying, he raised his eyes from the shelf. Tom was the manager and gave good advice, advice people trusted.

"You got somebody helping you put these pipes in?" Tom asked now.

"Looks simple enough," she told him. "Just hook them up under the sink, right?"

"Well, those old pipes can be hard to wrench loose. Might take somebody a little stronger to do the job."

"I'm stronger than I look," she said. "How much do I owe you?"

When Tom gave her the bag, he said, "Give us a holler, if you need some help, you hear."

"I'll be fine," she said, and headed for the door without once looking around at John Lucas.

About two hours later, John Lucas walked quietly around the back of her house and stood at the screen door, looking in at the woman sitting on the floor, in front of the kitchen sink. She was making a big racket, trying to loosen the pipes with a big wrench, and cussing.

"Need some help?" he asked.

"No!" she yelled.

He watched her give the wrench another tug, and smiled.

"Is this a," she grunted with another try, "social visit, or are you just here to make fun?"

He opened the creaky screen door, and walked into the kitchen.

"No social visit," he said, squatting down beside her, gently prying the wrench away from her hands. "Just thought you might need some help."

He gave the pipe joint a swift twist and took off the old pipe to be replaced, picked up the new one, but stopped then and looked at her. "May I?" he asked.

"It's all yours," she said. "The damn thing is all yours."

He finished the work and stood up.

"Is this where I am supposed to ask if you'd like a beer?

"I don't drink beer," he said, heading for the screen door. And without another word, he took off down the back steps and drove away.

Before the end of that fall, while the trees were still ablaze with glory, a number of people waited under a big, shady maple, anticipating the coming event. They whispered among themselves as they waited, "Would you have ever thought it?"

"Not after that outburst in the middle of Main Street."

"Or that time she "accidentally" dropped a can of paint on his toe, in Sam's."

"I liked it when he chased her in the field, mad as a hornet!" (snickering) "Till we couldn't see them anymore!"

"Remember when she rang the church bell over and over again, so everybody would look . . . after another fight when he knocked over the community horse trough?"

"Shhhhhhhh. Here they come!"

They came across the field running—holding hands, and laughing. She had on her grandmother's wedding dress, which she wore just as it was when lifted out of the box in the attic. The color—faded to a soft cream—blended beautifully with her red hair, laced now with wildflowers. And she wore the emerald earrings which had belonged to her mother.

He wore a jacket over a pair of crisp jeans, and a buttoned down, cream colored shirt. Afternoon light streaming through the multi-colored trees, made them look like part of some famous oil landscape. When they approached the crowd, they stopped laughing and running, and still breathless, tried to take on a somber manner.

"Dearly beloved," the preacher began . . .

Though he had been invited, Lester came only as far as the back trees, and peeked out from one of them. When the preacher finished talking, and John Lucas bent down to kiss Harna, Lester looked away. But afterward, when the fiddles started up and people were busy talking and dancing, Lester came shyly up to Harna and held out his hand, closed around some object. Harna smiled and put her hand under Lester's and when he opened his hand, a little rock, tinged with mountain gold, fell out. *Thank you,* Harna's eyes said, as she held the rock to her heart. Then she rubbed her fingers lightly and lovingly across his face, which caused a beatific smile to spread slowly under the fingers.

That night, in John Lucas' log cabin with only the light from the fireplace and a few candles, they lay in each other's arms in the big four-poster he had made himself.

"Did you marry me only to get the property back?" she asked, teasing.

"Of course," he whispered, drawing her to him again.

But while these words were said in jest, the question—now loosed—would stay with them. And it took seeing their own grandchildren born before either could put the incident totally to rest.

Ashley

Everybody knew her name. As soon as you said Ashley Clarke people remembered at least two or three movies right away, in which she had starred. She had been given a number of awards, feted at film festivals, even twice nominated for an Oscar, but in the last two years few scripts were sent to her and those had been for the category of "older woman." And she wasn't ready to own up, just yet.

She had, like all actors, been out of work periodically, but never this long. "Get your mind off of it," her agent Bert Howell suggested. "Do something different," he told her, rapping his fingers impatiently on the table. He was getting tired of the conversation, had more important things waiting than appeasing an aging actress. They were sitting around her pool, though no one was wearing a bathing suit. They had just finished having lunch at one of the green and white, umbrella-shaded tables.

"Like what?"

"Take a trip. take up a hobby. something, anything. Just for this period. A good script will come, it always does."

Ashley looked away. "What if it doesn't?" she said, then after a moment, turned back with a somber expression.

Bert was standing now. "It will. Trust me." And then he waved the air with his hand, "Don't bother. I'll let myself out."

He opened one of the huge double doors leading back into the house and walked down the long hall, toward the foyer. On the way, he stopped and retrieved his briefcase from the piano bench in the orange and pink hued living room. The piano, which no one played, was a showcase of photos, as was almost one entire wall—all of Ashley Clarke at various times in her career. Several framed awards were interspersed with the pictures. It seemed to Bert yet another photo had been added, but he had neither the time nor interest to look. A uniformed maid stood holding the door. "Thank you," Bert said, and hurried out to his car.

Ashley stared at the water in the pool until the sun reflected too strong. She didn't want to take a trip, she wanted to work. At least she did not want to take a trip unless she could glean something from it, as she had when working and doing research for a character. It enhanced and deepened the travel. But to take a trip just to take a trip? The idea bored. Especially without a man along, and she was not only between films, but between men as well. The last one had taken her to a whirl of parties—keeping her hand in, keeping her face "out there." She missed all that, almost as much as the work. It magnified the lull now. Well, no matter, she told herself, reminding that she was never long between men, that unlike films, there was always one out there, waiting in the wings.

She wished she could go back and see her grandmother, that's what would really help, she thought, but Granny had been gone almost ten years now. Ashley closed her eyes and thought of all the times her grandmother had given such sound advice. And—equally as important—all the times Granny had remained silent, and just listened. She thought of the old house then, and wondered if it was still there.

By that evening she had found out that the house was not sold, but had been left to her grandmother's spinster cousin, Dora Sanders, who had nursed Granny in her last years. Ashley picked up the phone and dialed the number.

"Dora? Dora Sanders? This is Ashley Clarke, Mavis' granddaughter." There was no reply. "We met once, at a family reunion."

"The glamor one?" Dora asked.

Ashley smiled. "Well, I'm . . . an actress." And after another silent moment, said, "Reason I'm calling is that I wondered if I could come and stay a few days in the house? I just . . . I've been thinking about Granny and would like to see the old house again."

A very long pause this time, then the voice—already raised a decibel or two by age—climbed even higher: "Coming here? When?"

"Well, not until you should say—and only if it is convenient for you."

"Mavis' granddaughter, you said?

"Yes. I'm the one who moved to California."

That seemed to register. "Well I'm not going to do anything fancy for this visit," she said, emphasizing the word fancy.

"I shouldn't expect you to. I'll only need a couple of days to be in the house. Take a few walks in the country, that sort of thing."

"It's a small town, you remember that. And plain. Walking's about the only thing you can do around here."

"Would this weekend be all right?"

"Come on. We'll just see."

High in the sky, flying toward North Carolina, Ashley's eyes were continually drawn to her reflection in the plane's small window. An elderly man shared the seats, and he sat near the aisle and appeared to be sleeping. She took out a mirror from her handbag, removed her dark glasses and looked seriously at the woman peering back. Then touched the sides of her eyes; crow's feet seemed to have deepened overnight. She put the mirror back. This time, when she turned to the window she saw herself in the arms of Joseph Grant, from an old movie—one of her earliest—about a plane crash. The plane was going down and they were kissing and whispering last minute endearments to each other.

"I love you," he had said. "I'll love you even more in eternity." Ashley let go the strap of her handbag, and brought her hand up to stroke the imaginary face. "I love you, too," she whispered now. Then, shutting out the sound of the old man snoring beside her, closed her eyes for the final kiss.

By the time the plane arrived and she managed to wave a taxi for the long ride to Sumpter County, she was tired. But just the sight of those hills, energized. It was dusk when the taxi pulled up at the house. The old house needed painting and appeared smaller than she remembered, but it seemed home to her. Ashley rolled down the window, breathing in the smog-free air, smiling. Someone was turning on the porch light now, and peering out from the curtained glass, bordering the side of the door. Dora presumably.

"I 'spect you'll want to go right to your room," Dora told her, "after that long trip. You go on up—second room to the right and I'll bring you a snack later."

Ashley put the suitcase down and looked around, almost overcome with memories of Granny.

"I assume you've had your dinner by now," Dora said, eyeing the too short skirt.

"I'll be fine," Ashley told her, and picked up the suitcase again and started up the stairs.

"I'll come up around eight o'clock with your snack. Then I'm in bed at nine. Nine o'clock sharp," she said to emphasize.

Though she would have preferred a warmer welcome, by the time Ashley had a hot bath and had consumed the snack, which was not a snack at all but enough for an adequate dinner, she felt better. She took out all her bottles and creams and lined them up on the dresser. One, with the improbable tag: "Guaranteed to erase fifteen years," was imported from France and cost ninety-five dollars an ounce. Ashley lifted the lid, but instead slowly put it back, and tugged at her hair, holding a cluster of blond strands out, away from one ear, looking underneath and frowning. Time for coloring again, she thought. After carefully smoothing the cream on her face, she did her upper arm exercises and got into bed. She noted Dora had left reading material on the night table: *History of Sumpter County*. It put her to sleep in ten minutes.

The next morning, as they sat around the kitchen table having breakfast, Ashley said, "Tell me about the Quakers. Granny was said to be a Quaker growing up, but I never heard much about them."

Dora seemed more intent on passing the food, than talking. When she saw that Ashley had a proper amount of everything on her plate, she answered, "That's because she married your grandfather, and went with him to his church."

"She must have missed going to her own."

"Well after your grandfather died and she moved back to this house to take care of her father, she started back to Quaker Meetings."

"I'm glad," Ashley said. Then, "Oh, I haven't had sausage and eggs all cooked together like this, since Granny died!"

They ate quietly for a while, then Ashley said with genuine feeling, "I *so* miss her."

"I 'spect you do," Dora said, though she was thinking of all the times Mavis had not heard from her granddaughter. She got up to take more biscuits out of the oven.

"Oh, no!" Ashley said when Dora placed a hot biscuit on her plate. "I have to watch my weight . . . It's a real fight!"

Dora sniffed and scooped up the biscuit. *A fight* . . . she repeated under her breath, sitting back down at the table.

"I feel Granny is still here," Ashley said, looking all around the kitchen. "I can almost see her standing at the counter, making a peach pie."

"I think I have some of her letters," Dora told her, spreading the blackberry preserves she put up last summer on her biscuit, "and old photos, too, that you might like to see."

"That would be wonderful!"

"We need to do these dishes, first. I like a neat house."

Later, Dora brought out boxes of old photos and set them all on the dining room table.

"You sit right here and if you have a question or two, I expect you'll find me. I need to get to my dusting. I'm not one to be idle."

The dining room was plain, as was the rest of the house, with only the essential furniture.

There were few pictures on the walls—landscapes, no portraits—and no framed photographs anywhere. Though it had always been somewhat plain, the house obviously had Dora's stamp.

Ashley made herself comfortable and opened the first box of photos. Many she had seen before, but one—a girl of about eight with long, blond pigtails, looked back at her with such a bright, expansive smile it startled. Ashley pulled the photo away from the others and studied the happy look carefully. Then she shoved it deep under all the rest.

When she got to the second box, she held up another photo. By this time Dora was dusting the dining room. "Is this . . ."

Dora stopped dusting and looked over Ashley's shoulder.

"Yes, that's her. Only about seventeen, eighteen years at the time."

"How *beautiful* she was."

"Your grandmother was the prettiest girl in the county."

"And this one?" Ashley said before the dusting should get started up again.

"Our old Quaker Meeting House."

"Is it still there?"

"Yes. I used to go on Sundays, but it's too far for me to drive now." She went back to the dusting. "Your great grandparents are buried out back, in the cemetery."

Ashley gave the photo another look. "A long way, you say?"

"No. About a half hour's drive is all. Still, too far for me."

"Could we go there? I'll drive—if you don't mind me driving your car."

"Depends on how I feel in the morning," Dora said. She left to continue her dusting in another room, but shortly came back to the door.

"You know the Quakers have silent meetings, don't you?"

"I think I read that, somewhere."

"Well I just want you to be prepared to sit still."

After Ashley had looked through all the photos—hunting Dora all over the house to ask questions— she said she thought she would take a walk. Just before she opened the screen door, she glanced at herself in the narrow, slightly cracked mirror on the wall and patted her hair. She was startled when Dora—as if she had just material-ized—said, "No need to primp around here. Nobody will be looking at you."

Walking down toward the creek, Ashley passed the peach orchard and then found the old swing, still hanging by ropes tied to the limb of an oak tree. She sat in the swing and pushed off, smiling. Then tried going higher and higher, looking up at the sun filtering through the tree limbs way above her head, her hair blowing straight back. Soon she was going so high her heart raced. She remembered stand-ing in the swing once as a girl, and projecting the swing almost over the top of a small nearby tree. When she raised her eyes up the rope with this memory, she became aware that the rope was dangerously tattered. She quickly slowed to a stop, hopped off, and headed again toward the creek.

When she got there, she sat on the side of the creek bank and lis-tened to the gurgle of the water. At one point she rubbed the ground with her hand, over and over, absently. Then she lay back and watched the clouds, shielding her eyes with her arm. She was not one to reflect on her life but something seemed prodding her, some uneasiness connected to the photos. The little girl in pigtails with the happy smile rose in her mind. She had almost grasped something while looking at the photo, some remnant of that innocent girl, who had loved to play with fireflies, putting them in a jar, fascinated by their lights blinking on and off. Instead, her mind saw the girl's smile fade only two years later, never to come back again quite like that, except on cue. *Too much water under that little girl's bridge now,* she told herself, dismissing it, and got up to continue her walk. She cut through the pasture this time, and on to the barn.

The old barn stood unused and in disrepair, and reminded Ashley of a scene in another of her early movies—a horror film— where she had walked into an old barn and said, "Hello. hello." She looked up at the old rafters now and said "Hello. hello." Almost immediately, two bats flew over her head and out of the barn. She was right after them, heading back toward the house, when she saw something in one of the upstairs windows. As she got closer, she realized it was Dora's face.

That afternoon Dora brought out the box of letters.

"These letters came to me after your mother died. But, rightfully," Dora continued, "they should go to you. The pictures, too." She put the box in Ashley's lap. "I think most were written to your grandfather, when he traveled out of the county on business."

Ashley took the letters out to the porch swing, to read. She opened the first letter. It seemed all about domestic endeavors—a broken water pipe she had managed to get repaired, and supervising the apple pickers. Then Ashley reread a part near the end, "*Oh Robert, I miss you so much. Especially our time at the end of the day when we'd sit on the side porch and watch the sunset. Come home soon. Love, Mavis.* And in the corner she had added, *Mind the light.*

Another letter admonished him for having two glasses of wine at a neighbor's Christmas party, "*when one would have been more than enough for anyone!*" She had again added in one corner, "*Mind the light.*"

As they sat in the parlor that evening—Dora sewing, Ashley sorting the letters, putting them in order by date—Ashley said, "What does 'mind the light' mean? I kept seeing it in Granny's letters."

Dora looked up from her sewing. "Means take care of your inner light—to mind your light. It's a Quaker saying."

"I kept seeing mention after mention of light in the letters. That saying and others."

Dora nodded and went back to her sewing. "It's important—the light."

The grandfather clock began to tell the hour. Eight long tones rang out in the room. Afterward, Ashley said in a dreamy voice, "All I ever wanted was to see my name in lights. That's the kind of light that drew me. I remember the first time I saw it on a marquee. I was there for the opening of a new movie, wearing a Cartier original. And when I stepped out of the car, a large crowd of people clapped. I looked up, just once, and there it was—*Ashley Clarke*—all lit up."

Dora stopped sewing. "Vanity," she said. "That's all it is, just plain vanity."

Ashley smiled. "Well if that's all it was, it still felt wonderful."

"Your grandmother told me your name used to be Abigail, before you went off to Hollywood. Said you were named after her."

"Yes, well, I had to change it, actually."

"Why?" Dora asked, her direct eyes staying fixed.

"Because Abigail was not what they wanted."

"Who?"

"The people who wanted to make me a star," Ashley told her.

"It's a good Quaker name," Dora said, and walked out of the room.

Ashley sighed and started putting all the letters back into the box. She was remembering a meeting, years ago, when the head of a major studio and her first agent were outlining plans for launching her career. They had agreed without a quibble that her name had to be changed.

"But, why?" Ashley asked.

"It's too 'girl next door,' and honey you sure aren't that."

"What am I, then?"

They both smiled. Then one said, "No Abigail ever looked like you."

They simply took my name away, she thought, as if a person's name didn't matter. *Discarded, like an old coat.* Ah, but when they slipped on the other one—the bright red one, the one with sequins— she had worn it as if she had never had another.

Upstairs, she stopped just outside of Dora's room. The door was partially open and Ashley peeked in to see her turning down the covers on her bed. There was a spartan look about the room—no dresser, just a small chest of drawers and a rocker placed near the window. The walls appeared to be completely bare.

"Will we go to the Quaker Meeting tomorrow? she asked.

The voice that answered still sounded a little distant. "We'll see."

Sitting on those hard wooden pews and feeling the morning sun on her shoulders in that unairconditioned Quaker Meeting took some getting used to, but Ashley finally settled down, took off her dark glasses, and closed her eyes. After some time passed, she even got used to the silence. She was imagining herself as a young, teenage Quaker, her feet twitching slightly under the long dress, her bonnet partially hiding her face and the eyes that began to look up, shyly, feeling the pull of his. One long look was all they dared, but oh, what they could do with their eyes—these silent Quakers! Ashley slowly tilted her head, her eyes connecting seductively with the imagined boyfriend. Then Dora shifted positions, and she quickly closed her eyes again. Her great grandmother could have been that teenager, she thought, and Granny herself could have sat in that very same pew as a girl growing up. Then a wave of sadness came over her so strong it startled; she was remembering Granny's illness which had occurred almost at the same time as her acting career was soaring. She had been doing one movie after another, in a whirlwind, told by her agent not to let the public forget.

"Keep that pretty face on the screen!"

And all of a sudden, Granny, her Granny, was gone, and it was one of Ashley's deepest regrets that she had not seen her before she died.

So many regrets, she thought now, three bad marriages—and afterward a number of affairs which came to the same end. Nothing ever working out except the acting—the only constant, the only thing in her life that had not left her. It began at ten, when her father left and she had turned slowly from her dolls, to *becoming* the dolls. She had found it easy to roll play; make believe was always better than reality. Then she was all caught up in it—or caught by it, she never quite figured that out. It gave her a semblance of stability in an unstable world. But later, as she played more and more characters on the big screen, her own sense of self had gradually faded. Life was never quite as real as when she was acting.

Now in that silent room of bowed heads and closed eyes, remorse persisted. No matter! she told herself, trying to still the thoughts, reminding herself that she had used all of it—that all had given her a reservoir of feelings to draw from, that all had been safely put into her films. Still the memories continued. Just when she thought she couldn't take anymore, someone shifted their feet and stood. The man only said a few words—a quote from the Bible it seemed—but they startled Ashley out of her reverie.

"Yet a little while is the light with you. Walk while you have the light," he said, then sat back down. What a strange people these Quakers were, she thought. No minister. and then this. Out of the blue! But the man's words reminded her of Granny's letters and her writing about the light. Then a photo of Granny found in the boxes— the last one taken—came to mind. Signs of the illness invading her body were already evident. Ashley had held the photo next to her heart, and with eyes misting, realized the real reason she had come back to the old house—to say goodbye.

Her somber mood prevailed after the Meeting was over. She put the dark glasses back on, though no one seemed to have noticed her. They were walking down the steps.

"You said my great grandparents were buried here," she said to Dora. "Would you show me?"

Dora led the way behind the Meeting House, where some graves dated back to the 1700s. When they reached the far side of the cemetery, Dora stopped. "Here. I believe this is it."

Ashley looked down but saw nothing but two mounds.

"Your great grandparents are buried right here."

"But there are no stones."

"Early Quakers were not encouraged to have markers."

"How do you even know for sure who is buried here?"

"All the spaces are documented in the Meeting records," Dora said. "But they are my ancestors, too, remember."

Ashley frowned at the simple mounds.

"Why on earth did they have no markers!"

Dora sighed. "It was their way of keeping themselves from being prideful or vain."

Ashley rolled her eyes upwards. "Do the Quakers still *do* it?"

"A few. It's *very* rare, now. Many get cremated today."

"Granny has a marker."

"Well she is buried next to your grandfather, in the big cemetery."

"But what about these other people," Ashley said, gesturing with her arm, looking at several identical, small, flat stones on a few nearby graves. "They have markers." She walked over to one; it was so old she could barely read the dates.

"Some of the Quakers did not comply," Dora said. "But most did. They believed that all people were equal and there was no need for a fancy stone, or *any* stone, really." Dora added, "Plain coffins, too. Mostly ash or pine. And the expense saved was to be given to the poor."

A bevy of crows flew overhead. When their caws diminished, Dora said, "We are the last, you know. On this side of the family." Ashley just looked at her; the idea had not occurred.

"Everybody gone from either the wars, old age, or illness," Dora said. "'Cept us."

The idea shocked Ashley silent. *Were they all gone? Uncle Harry, too?* But now she remembered a phone call received in Italy, where she was filming a musical—the days crammed with singing lessons. Though she had wired flowers, the call regarding Uncle Harry had barely registered.

As they walked back to the car, Ashley asked Dora, "Would *you* do it? Have no marker?"

Dora waited a while before answering. The buzz of a June bug mingled with their soft footsteps on the gravel walkway. "I'm studying on it," she said.

Ashley was silent as they drove back. The tone set in the Meeting stayed with her. Then a thought came into her mind so clear it was almost as if Dora had suggested it. What if *she* decided to have no marker on her own grave? That would be the real news maker, not just the fact that she had died. She imagined the newspaper blurb: *Ashley Clarke, renowned actress, will be buried in an unmarked grave at her request. "Like my Quaker ancestors."* The thought at first amused her—then absorbed.

The phone rang over the squeak of the screen door, as soon as they got back. It was Bert, telling her that Paramount wanted her for a film "tailor made for you!" Then went on to tell her that she must come back right away, that they needed to be in a meeting in the morning.

"This is it, Ashley. The one you've been waiting for." And when she asked, he said, "Yes, yes, the age is perfect. You'll look good in this one, babe!"

"No time for lunch," she told Dora. "I must leave as soon as possible. A wonderful film offer!"

"Well I'll make you a sandwich, anyway," Dora said, unimpressed. "You can take it with you," she told her, walking off toward the kitchen.

Ashley opened her mouth to say lunch would probably be available on the plane, but then thought better of it and hurried upstairs to pack.

"Thank you for everything," Ashley said at the door, already eyeing the awaiting taxi.

Dora nodded and then surprised Ashley by reaching out and giving her a slightly awkward hug. "Take care of yourself," she said. Then added, "Abigail."

"You, too," Ashley told her, smiling.

Dora gave her the little brown bag containing the sandwich. "You could write once in a while."

Ashley handed her suitcase over to the driver, who swooped it up and headed to the taxi. "I might just do that," she said, her hand waving backwards, taking the porch steps by twos.

The taxi had only gone a short distance when Ashley took out her mirror and looked at herself, lifting her chin and checking from different angles. "Good bones," she whispered. "I'll *always* have that." Then she remembered the touch-up her hair needed, and her mind raced.

So much to do! She reached for her purse to get out a notebook for her list. The brown bag containing the sandwich sat next to the purse. . . .

"Someone gave me a sandwich to take," she said to the driver, "but I have to watch my weight. Would you like it? I'm sure it's quite good."

"Thanks," the driver said, and she handed it over the back of the seat.

When the taxi turned off on the back road to the airport, they soon passed a small cemetery hugging the side of the road and the memory of the old Quaker cemetery came back. Ashley thought again what a stroke it would be to have no marker. But she knew she'd never do it. Instead she saw a huge stone, a proper epitaph, a place where people from everywhere could come and pay their respects.

Vidella

Vidella stood in the hall, looking at herself in the mirror, and adjusted the brim of her hat. The hat was new, and although most women had stopped wearing them, she did not feel properly dressed without one—at least on certain occasions. The dress was not new, not for some years, but its classic design and the fact that her trim figure stayed basically the same, kept it in her closet. One more glance in the mirror, this time holding a small mirror from her pocketbook to reflect from the larger one, told her she was ready.

"Slade . . . Slade!" she hollered up the steps. "We're going to be late!"

"You don't have to yell . . . I'm coming."

Vidella walked out on the porch and stood near the far end, trying to feel out the day, glad the children were at her mother's. She looked at the sky—a few dark clouds hovered toward the west, but basically things looked good, with the air clear and not too hot. Of course with those clouds, things could change later on. Then she sighed. Funerals were burdensome. And this one—the one she knew she would have to sit contained, with her insides tearing her up—was going to be especially so.

Slade came out with his coat on his arm and locked the front door.

"You know you've got to wear that jacket."

"Vidella, it's a warm day, expecting to get warmer. I'll put the thing on when I get there."

In the car, she looked out the window and turned quiet. They passed the barn, the rows of corn and peanuts, and still they had not left their property—not until they passed the meadow that sat still and pristine under the old oaks. She noted the light filtering through the trees in rays, and it seemed to her as if some unseen thing were being highlighted in that open area. Then a sob stabbed her so hard, she gasped. When Slade looked over at her, she feigned a cough.

"Not getting a cold, I hope?"

"No. . . ."

She continued to look out the window, and he went back to driving. How on earth will I do this thing? she asked herself. How will I go through with it?

It was a grave-side service. When they drove through the big cemetery gates, Slade counted the cars and whistled. "Would you look at that . . . gonna have to park around the side, looks like."

The accident had shocked them all. A drunk truck driver taking a wrong turn through their town—and within seconds one of their own, gone.

She was looking out the window on his side now, noting the large group gathered under the canopy. Why wouldn't there be a crowd? Johnny was special.

Before they found a seat, Slade whispered, "Do you want to view the body?"

. . ."Yes," she answered, though in her heart she was saying no, no, no!

They stood just a moment in front of the open casket. Vidella held her handkerchief so tight in her hand that her nails hurt her palm, then slowly moved her eyes up the padded satin lining to the face. *Johnny. Johnny. What have they done to you.* The shock of seeing him with all that pancake makeup and that eerie, half smile they had put on him, made her heart sink. It had been a while since she looked directly at him; after it ended, whenever they had to be at the same occasion they looked away, or barely spoke. It magnified the present moment. This awful bareness, she thought. But even so, something still sparked, still had the power to move her. And it was almost suffocating her now. *I loved you Johnny. I loved you hard.*

Slade took her arm and led her down the side to two folding chairs on the far left.

The minister cleared his throat and began. But Vidella didn't hear a word he said, only the song of a bird high up in a tree nearby. She didn't need a minister to tell her about Johnny; she knew all there was to know about him. Knew, especially, the feel of those thighs, the strength of those arms. The bird's shrill song changed tempo and her mind went back to one night in Johnny's law office, when she was supposed to be at a PTA meeting and he was supposed to be working late—with the blinds closed tight and the two of them on the couch, trying to be quiet.

They were all standing now, and singing something. Slade moved the hymnal over so she could see it, too. The voices all around her sounded unreal, more like a soundtrack from a movie, but when she heard Slade's off-key voice begin to sing out beside her, it brought her back.

When they sat back down, she listened for the bird again, but only heard a faint trail as it moved further and further through the trees, and away.

The casket was partially visible between the couple sitting in front of them, and her eyes lit there. The minister was talking about "This . . . our last sleep," and she thought, *How many times did I watch him sleeping?* A sob caught in her throat, and she coughed again, several times.

Slade quickly looked her way.

"I'm okay," she said, keeping her eyes down. Then pointed at her throat. "This cold."

She could see Alice and the children, sitting on the front row—just the back of their heads, she was thankful for that. The woman blowing her nose never had an inkling. Not once during the whole of it did she even guess. And though Slade had questioned her, especially when she stayed much too long, he had never shown any sign that he knew, either. But then, Johnny was his good friend.

Later, as they drove away, she looked back once, and her eyes concentrated on the mound of dirt, just behind the casket, and she thought, "By nightfall, all that dirt will be smoothed over." She stifled another sob.

"When we get home, you need to do something about that cold."

"Yes. . . ."

"I'll fix you a hot toddy."

"I think I'd like to just go to bed."

"The toddy, first, would help."

Vidella stayed on the porch while he went in to make their drinks. She was sitting in the rocking chair with her hat on her lap, looking out toward the meadow. *Ah, Johnny,* she whispered, shaking her head. Then, of a sudden, it came to her that his name would never leave her now, but remain paused, fixed in time, claiming a part of her forever. And that the sound of a train whistle in the night, or the long hoot of an owl, or the rising song of cicadas in summer grasses, might suddenly bring it forth. The thought stopped her slow rocking.

Slade brought the drink out to her on the porch. The clouds had moved closer, and the air was thick and humid.

"Wouldn't you rather go inside?" he asked.

"No . . . no. I'm fine here."

He swirled the ice around in his drink, and looked out toward the meadow, too. "Guess I've lost my old fishing partner," he said, and took a long drink.

Vidella reached up and squeezed his hand.

"Never was good at losing people," he told her.

"None of us are," she said, her voice flat.

He reached down and patted her on the shoulder. Then stepped a bit to the side and sat on the banister in front of her, still looking out, beyond them. "Thought I lost you, one time," he said, and jiggled the ice again and took another long drink.

She stopped rocking again. "When I had the miscarriage?" she asked.

"No . . . not then." He rubbed his chin and took a deep breath. A dragon fly tried to light on his glass. "No, it was another time."

She sat very still and waited. Thunder could be heard in the far distance.

He turned and looked back at her and she saw his eyes were red and brimming, and the sadness in them broke her heart. He didn't say anything, just looked at her, and she had an overwhelming urge to get up and hold him. But, still, she sat and waited. When it seemed neither of them could bear that look any longer, he turned away.

"It was when Johnny was still with us," he said, looking out over the fields.

She held her breath.

A long time seemed to pass before he turned back again with all that visible agony and blurted out, "The two people I loved best in all the world!"

"Ah, Slade . . . Slade. You knew, and you never told me."

He turned away, and shook his head over and over again, his shoulders drooping like someone had hit him in the stomach. "I knew," he said.

She looked down at her cup. "I'm sorry. I'm so very sorry," she said, and meant it. But she only meant she was sorry she had hurt him, not that she was sorry about Johnny.

"Are you?" he asked, and his voice had some control now.

She didn't answer, rather put her head back and started rocking again. She vaguely noted dirt daubers had made a home in the ceiling of the porch.

He went into the house and made another drink. She heard him getting ice out of the refrigerator. She went in, too, and walked up the steps, feeling very, very, tired. She hung up her dress, then lay on the bed in her slip and watched the ceiling fan go around and around and heard nothing but its soft whirring.

Presently, Slade came in and began to remove his suit pants and hang them up. He took off his shirt and draped it over the chair. Then he came and sat down on the bed next to her, and removed his shoes and socks. He stayed that way, very still, in his shorts, just staring at the wall. She was turned to the other wall, with one arm folded under her head, her eyes open. Neither spoke. There was only the whirring sound of the fan.

Finally, she took a deep breath and sighed, "It's hard sometimes," she said. "This living."

"I followed you once . . . to Raleigh," he said, still looking at the wall. "Sat outside the motel and waited, just to see how long you'd stay."

"Oh, God, Slade." One tear fell down her cheek.

"Finally, I left . . . before you did."

"I was crazy," she said, though the kind of craziness she meant she could never tell him about. Crazy with desire, pushed up hard against a wall, Johnny tearing at her clothes, she at his, both breathless, and that kissing . . . that wild, wild, kissing that went on and on, and all over her body. *Johnny, Johnny . . . we were crazy, we really were.*

It had been this craziness that had finally forced her to bring an end to it—the fear that her mind would turn in the same wild direction as her body. This, and gut-wrenching guilt.

"I'd go fishing with him and think of ways to kill him," Slade said.

"You never said a word to him, did you?"

"No."

"Why?"

"It seemed something out of my control. Something . . . that scared me quiet." He threw the one sock left in his hand, to the corner.

Tears were rolling down her cheeks now. "I am so terribly sorry," she told him.

"It's over now," he said, and the defining quality in his voice caused her to bite her lower lip hard, not knowing which way he meant the statement. Then he sighed and lay down beside her. There was a long, still moment before he turned toward her and moved his body into a spoon-like position, though still some distance from hers. They stayed that way, both looking toward the window, as large raindrops began to ping, one by one, against the pane.

The clouds from the west had moved overhead, filling the room with shadows.

Suddenly the rain began streaking the window in sheets, and she sensed Slade's body moving closer. The movement was accompanied by a long sigh, full of anguish and surrender. Then he put one—very tentative—arm around her shoulder. She listened hard to the loud pounding on the roof, closed her eyes and let the sound pour over her—releasing all of it now, to be washed and washed by the rain.

Jake

Jake McCoy was sly, and slippery as a green back toad. Something about his eyes told you this, just before you shook his hand. You just didn't trust the man. Three words came to the surface of your mind, *Watch your back.*

He came into town the same night the cold weather arrived, almost as if he brought it.

I woke up the next morning in my place over the store, looking out to see all that grey wintery sky, and noted a beat up looking station wagon across the street, parked in front of the Gaslight Hotel. Even then, something said caution to me. Nicked myself shaving, thinking about it.

First thing I did was go downstairs and get the heat going in the store. Upstairs, where I lived, it didn't matter—I could take a little cold—but when people came in to buy groceries they wanted to be comfortable. Later on, when I turned around from stocking the shelves and saw him standing there, it startled me—most folks made a little noise coming in. When he introduced himself and stuck out his hand, that's when I got the feeling of unrest. Those half-lidded eyes would look at you, then slide off sideways and come back again, as if he was thinking hard about something else.

He asked me about the town, just general stuff—you know, where is a good place to eat, and so forth. As if he didn't know a thing about Thomasville. Then he came out with it.

"The Watson's still live around here?"

"Jed Watson?" I asked. Nobody had mentioned the man in years.

"Yeah."

"He died. Some time ago."

The eyes slipped sideways for a moment. Then he asked, "What about the daughter, Judy?"

Right then was when I should have excused myself and gone on into the back and phoned her up. But I went on and told him, "She's still here. She and her mother."

"You know where 'bouts they live?"

"Same place," I told him, not wanting to give out any more information.

But he just said, "Thanks," and went on his way.

I pondered whether to call Judy when I saw his station wagon moving on in the right direction, but then thought better of it. None of my business, I said to myself.

At nine o'clock, Judy came in, just like always, and took up her place behind the counter. I studied her expression, but it didn't tell me anything.

"A man was here," I said. "Asking about your family."

She looked up.

"Asking about you," I said.

"Who?"

"Said his name was Jake McCoy."

She changed expression then, right quick. "What'd you tell him?" Her voice came out faint.

"Told him your daddy had passed on, but you and your mama were still living here."

She looked away then, and busied herself with straightening the shelves. I took that to mean the conversation had ended, as far as she was concerned. I didn't push it.

All day long Judy seemed edgy, and once went into the back to call her mama. I knew that 'cause I could hear most of the conversation.

"Mama, Jake's here." Something about her worried tone of voice, made me stop rattling papers and strain to hear.

"I don't know. He came into the store this morning, asking about . . . the family." Whispers now. "Yes, he knows daddy died." Her voice got even lower. "Don't be rude, if he comes. Wait until I get home. I'll take care of it."

When she came back in, she said, "I'm going to need to leave early today. Need to see about mama."

"She sick?" I asked, but mainly just to make her think I didn't hear the conversation.

"No, but I need to take care of something."

"Sure," I told her. "You just go on early."

All my life I tried to stay out of people's business. But this one nagged me. There was a mystery in it. I looked across the street and saw that the station wagon was still gone.

Later that night, I was lying in bed reading when I heard—my ears were tuned to it—the sound of a car stop, and then a car door slam, hard. I turned off the light and peeked out the window and saw the station wagon and then a figure walking up the steps of the Gaslight Hotel. Something about the way he jerked the door open made me feel he was mad. I eased on back to bed, but didn't turn the light back on, just laid there looking at the ceiling.

Next morning, Judy was a little late and seemed flustered. Couldn't keep her mind on anything all day, just kept looking across the street.

So she knows, I thought. She knows that's where he's staying. Every time a customer came into the store she'd jump.

Finally, I said, "You all right today, Judy?"

"Yes," she told me. But there had been a long sigh before her answer, and I looked at her carefully. "How's your mama?"

"Mama's fine," she said and went on to the area where we kept the cold cuts and began straightening the case.

I kept my eye on her most of that day. Nothing new about that, though. I usually kept my eyes on Judy, she was hard not to look at. Hair shining like a new penny, and the sweetest smile you ever saw— at least until this Jake fella came into town. First time we worked together her very presence made me tongue tied—the way she moved in her clothes, and that soft voice.

And something else, a kind of sadness that came up to the surface every now and then, just made me want to put my arms around her. But I never did, of course, 'cept in my dreams.

That night after she left, I closed up and went to Hank's Restaurant on the corner, to get my supper. Right after I ordered, I saw the station wagon pull up at the hotel, and it was not long before Jake McCoy walked into the restaurant and sat down, four booths away. I kept on chewing my roast beef and looking out the window, as if I didn't see him walk in.

"Number four," he told the waitress in a voice that said that was what he wanted and no two ways about it. Gladys wrote it down on the pad. "Coffee?" she asked. I watched the two of them over the rim of my cup.

He smiled up at her then, and I felt I was looking at a whole different person. "I'd rather have bourbon," he said.

Gladys smiled back. "Me, too, but it's not on the menu." They both laughed.

Now, I've known Gladys to be a quiet type. Not given to talking much, but here she was, joking with a perfect stranger. I just kept my head down, finishing my dinner, while all this was going on.

Usually Gladys came over to see if I needed any more coffee or anything, but not this night. I had to wave her over twice. But Jake McCoy didn't seem to have that problem.

When I got up to leave, I nodded to the man and he nodded back, and Gladys finally noticed me enough to say, "Come back soon."

Outside, as I walked by the window I saw them with their heads close, as if in a deep conversation.

That night, the station wagon woke me up, screeching to a halt in front of the hotel. I was mad as hell when I jerked up the blind to see Jake, wobbling up the steps of the Gaslight.

Next day, Judy was so quiet you hardly knew she was there. About 2 PM Jake McCoy pushed open the door hard, and the bell made her turn around. I saw her face then and decided I didn't know a thing about women. It was as if she was relieved to see him. As if she had waited for this. He walked over and leaned against the counter. I made myself like a fly on the wall and watched.

"What time you get off?" he asked in a slow, teasing kind of voice, raising his eyes up to meet hers. I saw that they were bloodshot, but she apparently saw something else.

She said, "Around 4:30," and smiled really sweet.

"I'll be . . . home," he told her.

"I'll think about it," she said.

He grinned. "Think hard," he told her, and walked on out the door.

That was one of the worst afternoons I'd ever spent in my life. Not only worrying about Judy getting herself mixed up with somebody most of us wouldn't pass the time of day with, but worrying about something else, too, something that had to do with me. I was trying to figure out how he could close in so quickly, when I would have given anything to have her look at me, like that. I was trying to figure out how in the devil I had waited so long to let Judy know how I felt about her.

The clock became the most important thing in the store that day. I just kept looking up at it, and dreading the time she would close the door behind her and go across the street. The way I figured it, I had only three hours to make my move.

"How's your mother?" I asked, after the store became empty for a while.

"She's okay."

"You seemed worried, the other day."

"Well . . . we got that settled."

"Something about that Jake fella?"

She looked straight at me. I'd never brought up personal things before. Like I said, I try to stay out of folks' business, so this must have surprised her as much as it did me.

"He . . . I knew him a long time ago."

"Your mama, she knew him, too?"

Judy looked like she was weighing the question—whether she would answer it or not. Finally she said, "Mama is hard on people, sometimes," and looked away.

I just kept at it. "I thought your mama was straight shooting, that's what I always liked about her . . . said what she thought."

"Yeah, well, sometimes she says too much."

A customer came in then, and started talking about the weather. I thought the man would never get what he wanted and leave.

Afterward, I took it up again. "This Jake McCoy . . . what does he do for a living?"

Judy frowned at me, and I wished I could take the words back. But then she said slowly, as if she liked saying it, "He says he's into cattle now."

"Must have help," I said, "to be able to get away. Must have somebody doing the feeding and all."

"Yes," she said, but it was as if she was wondering about that, herself. "Course, if he's not too far away, he could go back and take care of things."

"He's . . . living in Manchester," she said.

"Oh, well, that's too far, then. Yeah, he'd have to have help," I told her.

The clock on the wall was saying a quarter to four. Judy had gone off to get more bread from the back—seemed we could never stock enough bread. The phone rang about then, and I heard her answer it, "Mama, don't call me at work," she said. There was a long pause. "You've got him all wrong, mama." Then a longer pause. "Look, I can't talk about that now. And I'm going to be late coming home tonight. Mama . . . Mama!. I haven't even said it was with him! What? Oh, you know everything don't you, you know everything about everybody!"

Then a pause so long I stopped breathing to hear. "I don't believe that," Judy said, her voice was calm now as if she was listening in spite of herself. "How could that . . . No, he would never do that."

I went over and put the closed sign on the door so no one would come in.

"I don't care what daddy told you, I knew him a long time. And I know he is honest. I gotta go now, mama. Don't call me back."

I jerked the sign off the door, and made sure I was working over the inventory when she returned. I just kept my head down, figuring. Or, looking like I was figuring.

In a minute, she said, "That was mama." I looked up and nodded and went back to the figures, trying to show disinterest.

"She thinks Jake is a con artist. Can you imagine! Picked that up after talking to him for only about twenty-five minutes. Told him as much, too!"

I remembered the angry slamming of the car door, the first night he arrived. "Your mother is a smart woman, Judy," I said. "And she cares about you."

"No, she is a nosey woman, that's what. And she believed everything daddy ever told her."

I went back to the books, again.

"Daddy . . . stopped us from dating, years ago," she said, her voice forlorn now. "We were real tight, Jake and me. But daddy said Jake was destined for trouble."

I looked up then. "Was he?"

"No! Look at him now, with cattle and everything! I don't know why mama can't believe it."

"Well, you could call her bluff, if you wanted to," I said in an off-hand manner while filing some papers. "Just by calling the nearest livestock market to Manchester, and asking about Jake."

Judy didn't say anymore, but shortly I heard her on the phone again, and raised my head.

"Could you tell me if a Mr. McCoy uses your livestock market for his cattle? Mr. Jake McCoy, from Manchester. Yes, I'll wait."

Then I heard her again, "You don't have anyone by that name on your records? You're sure? You must have! It's very important!"

I could hear her tapping her foot on the floor, impatiently.

"What? Yes . . . yes, I'll talk to them."

There was quite a long pause, then, "I see."

I heard her put the phone down without another word.

When she walked back in, I kept my head down over my papers. At first she stayed quiet. Started sweeping the floor, but it seemed as though she was sweeping the same spot, over and over again. It magnified the swishing sound of the broom—back and forth, back and forth, like a pendulum of a clock. I watched her from the corner of my eye. Occasionally she would stop and look toward the hotel with a frown on her face. Finally, she came out with it.

"I always knew he'd come back someday . . . used to dream about it. Even though Daddy said he was living up in Canada, to escape the war." She was leaning on the broom and all that sadness I had first perceived, was in her face now.

"Somebody in that office knew a Jake McCoy from Manchester," she said. "Came to the phone to tell me Jake was never into cattle, and the last they heard he had changed his name again. Said he tended to go off and change his name, all the time."

I didn't say anything.

"Why in the world would someone want to take on different names?" she said, but it was more like she was asking it of herself. "When a name is what you kept. A name is what said you were you."

She was getting her coat now, and I looked quick at the clock. Four-twenty five. My heart sank. What could a man do in five minutes?

She got to the door and turned back to me, her face full of anguish, "Why, a name is just about the most important thing there is!"

I watched her close the door, then I went to the window. She was still standing out front, looking up at the Gaslight Hotel. I moved back a bit but stayed there, at the corner of the window, whispering to myself like an idiot, *Don't do it. Don't do it.*

When I saw her get into her car, I started breathing again. She was driving off in the direction of home. I went and put the Closed sign back in the window. Then, on impulse, I opened the door and walked out on the sidewalk a bit, and looked up at my sign. The large yellow letters formed "Powell's Grocery," and they defined me. I was proud of the name, and the store built from scratch.

I started to go in, but instead turned and looked up at the sign again. Now that I knew how important a man's name was to her, it gave me the confidence I had lacked.

It was this that would win her over, I told myself. I knew it in my bones.

Credits and Awards

"Myrtice" was adapted by the author into a stage play entitled, "Woman of Property," which won a GIGA Moondance International Film Festival award in 2006.

"Solomon" was published in *In Good Company,* Live Wire Press, 2005.

"Harna" won Best Short Story in the 2008 Moondance International Film Festival. It was later adapted into a screenplay by the author, entitled "The Land," which won Best Feature Screenplay Award in the 2009 Moondance International Film Festival.

"Rosa" won a semi-finalist Flash Fiction Award, *New Millennium* magazine, 2015.

"General B.D. Martin" appeared in "Pettijohn Junction" which was published in *In Good Company,* Live Wire Press, 2016.

"Casey" was published in *Short Stuff* magazine in 2000.

"Burl" won an Irene Leache Literary Festival award at the Chrysler Museum, Norfolk Va. in 1995.

Shirley Wilson lives in Newport News, Virginia and is a writer of short stories, plays, screenplays and essays. Most recent credit was being named one of the screenplay finalists in the 2016 Richmond International Film Festival. A radio drama, produced by Shoestring Radio Theater, was aired on over one hundred PBS radio stations in 2013.

She has had several plays produced in Virginia, as well as two in Canada, and her short stories have been published in literary journals and national magazines. One short story published in *Redbook* brought a three-year film option. Essays have been published in both regional publications, and one anthology. She has received three fellowships from the Virginia Center for Creative Arts (VCCA).

In 1993, she won the Governor's Screenplay Award, presented at the Virginia Film Festival in Charlottesville.